DOMINION

An Apocalyptic Epic in Seven Books

BOOK III

TRYST

by

Compasse

Sacrata Dei Press

A Division of The Compasse Corporation

Front Cover Art: *Beckoning Fate*, by Ben Hamrick

Back Cover Art: *Paradise Lost 2*, by Gustave Doré

Printed in the United States of America

For John Karol Mary, Jacinta Christopher, Gianna Anthony,
& David Guadalupe;

I pray that I may one day see the marvelous vision that you now
embrace…

Authors' Note

Can forgiveness exist without betrayal?

Betrayal seems to be a universal theme that has run throughout the history of civilization, and even today it is perhaps the most common soul-injuring experience we have with one another. Whether in literature or historical account, from Adam's choice against an all-loving God, to Brutus' plotting against Julius Caesar, to Judas Iscariot's conspiring against Jesus Christ; betrayal seems to exist at the center of our human experience, clinging like a parasite to the oft-misunderstood reality of love.

Who has lived even a few years into adolescence without acquiring the wounds of a friendship that ended with a seemingly uncharacteristic and unforgivable act *against* that relationship? The interior devastation our spirits experience often quickly transforms into the seeds of hatred; revealing the curious truth that the opposite of love is not hatred, but *indifference*. Why? Because hatred finds its origins in a love and trust betrayed. Nonetheless, within this interior maelstrom of the injured, the essence of love remains, though it has been tainted. If allowed to fester unchallenged, these wounds inevitably mutate into something much darker.

Why else would forgiveness be such a powerful reality? It is a concept that seemingly transcends the tenets of good reason and self-preservation. It is the foolishness of willfully providing the source of our wounding with a clear opening to engage in further, and even deeper, harm! It is inarguably *against* nature, defying the very precepts of "survival of the fittest." Yet in its purest form, forgiveness draws us into an even deeper relationship with our one-time betrayer, forging a bond more steadfast than existed even before the injury. Truly, an authentic mutual forgiveness makes us *more* vulnerable, yet paradoxically more secure within the healing union.

It is true, sometimes *perceived* betrayal can be more the result of a misunderstanding rather than a deliberate act against the beloved—and these situations can be even more devastating in the sense that forgiveness is less likely to be sought when one believes they have not truly offended. In these circumstances, the past experience and interior wounding of the "betrayed" directly impacts their ability and desire to sort through the misconstruction. Sadly, it seems more often than not, our premature reaction of offense to being accused—along with our impulse for self-preservation—often result in an act of counter-betrayal, further manifesting a dark rift in the relationship. In this scenario, where now *both* parties have caused offense, "good reason" would suggest separation and dissolution of the relationship, would it not?

Still, in the more classic definition of betrayal, we find a person who has, perhaps in a moment of weakness, responded to a perceived opportunity with a self-serving act. This response in itself is understandable; in essence, it is motivated by our more primal fallen natures. Yet without the antidote we call forgiveness, which begins with contrition and is often completed through an act of reparation, we truly cannot live in authentic relationships with others, and even our so-called sentiments of love become self-deceptive forms of ego-fulfillment. But to be clear (lest the author be accused of cynicism), I believe that love *does* exist in our world, even if only in forms possessing varying degrees of imperfection. Love is that very desire for the good of another, even at substantial cost to oneself, which has also manifested itself throughout history and within the day-to-day human experience in acts of deep altruism… and great sacrifice. While betrayal is always an act *against* love, an authentic love can never be fully extinguished by it.

Yes, authenticity is key here! The superficial forms of reconciliation often promoted in our current pop social psychology today between spouses, groups, and even nations focus less on healing wounds than on covering them up. As St. Francis de Sales stated, "a slow cure is a sure cure"; true healing *must* begin as the source of the wound, and it is often through a heroic—even "unreasonable"—act of love and courage that this is achieved.

In conclusion (though really, are we not just getting started?) in dealing with the topic of betrayal and forgiveness, our initial instinct is to reflect upon those times when we have served as a victim. Yet as we attempt to grasp that elusive honest objectivity that often goes along with self-reflection, would not the better path be to ask when we ourselves have played the part of the betrayer? We deal here with a great mystery, and though another's act of betrayal may provide objectively sound reason for our dismissal of the betrayer from our lives, as any soul who has lived through such an experience can attest, unforgiveness comes with a price.

- *Compasse*

...From Phoenix

Eleven years had passed since that fateful night of Tobias' slaying, with the subsequent escape of Vanya Ciotola and her nephew, Jesse. The world has changed dramatically in this period, yet following the Second Depression and a period of isolationism, the United States of America has begun to emerge from the ashes under the leadership of the much maligned, yet unwavering, President Hugh Jennings Lang.

Jonathan Corban Storm, the new identity adopted by Jesse thanks to his grandfather Nesterov's connections, is now rapidly approaching graduation from high school. Despite tormenting dreams of his past, it has been a gratefully uneventful season in his life, even offering some sense of "normalcy," living together with his Aunt Vanya, who has taken on the public identity of his mother. Though having a deep affection for his grandmother, the faithful Annie D., Jonathan finds himself grateful that the majority of his grandfather's time is spent not with him and his aunt, but in a relentless obsession to track down Harold Freeman, an informant within his own circle who has turned against the syndicate, now hiding under the protection of the FBI's Witness Protection Program.

Jonathan has excelled in all areas of academics and athletics, yet he has forged a friendship over the past six years with the free-spirited and irreverent Nathan Page, a boy with his own shadowed past. Nathan is at the opposite end of just about every spectrum there is when compared to Jonathan, yet their camaraderie is seemingly indissoluble.

A freak car accident, where Jonathan miraculously (and unwittingly) heals a dying child, ends up being the first of several events that slowly strip away the layers of secrecy which have served as Jonathan's protection. Luther, who despite his success in uniting the major pagan and occult sects under his leadership, has never relented in his pursuit of his son, Jesse. An odd providence, bearing a darker source, has allowed him to slowly close in on the boy's whereabouts.

For his part, Luther is pleasantly surprised to learn that his tryst from years before with the dim Delilah Hagarot has provided him another son, Samuel, a half-brother to Jesse. The multitalented, but seemingly disturbed Samuel strives for his father's approbation while harboring resentment towards the favored son, Jesse. Nonetheless, Samuel desperately yearns for a true family.

Alexandre Nesterov finds his world further decaying after he is unsuccessful in preventing the execution of the head of his syndicate, Danny Caputo. Rumors abound that Nesterov even intended the demise of Caputo, and an internal war breaks out within the syndicate. Nesterov is then betrayed by one of his own, the ambitious and opportunistic chain-smoking Mikhail Ostankino. Following the murder of his son, Yerik, Nesterov goes into hiding but then emerges to form a fragile truce with the other crime syndicates—including

Ostankino—forging an alliance under their shared goal: the public demise of the mole Harold Freeman and his entire family.

Jonathan's world begins to unravel as Luther attempts to seduce him into his own unholy alliance, promising a shared dominion over this plane of existence, while offering an opportunity to "make things right" in the world. The Illumini, Luther's coterie of semi-immortal men of historical influence, grow impatient with Jonathan's vacillation on accepting his birthright as "The Anointed." Luther assures them that Jonathan's own free act to join him will be of much greater value than a forced union, but pledges that he himself will destroy his seed if Jonathan does not accept this destiny.

As Jonathan's interior struggles continue to intensify, he once again finds solace in music, where he, Nathan, Simon Wilson, and Joey Escario discover a mystifying chemistry among them and form a band, The Phoenix. A "chance" break provides the crew with an opportunity to perform before a large audience, the last step in realizing their dreams of emerging onto the world stage of fame and influence.

Yet the boys have learned that there is a competitor to the band in becoming the music industry's "next big thing." Two men claiming to work for a man named Jimi T. Expo corner the vulnerable Joey Escario, blackmailing him into participating in their diabolical scheme. On the night of The Phoenix's breakout concert, circumstances push Nathan and Jonathan into an unanticipated and undesired full disclosure of their respective pasts and identities; Nathan is the son of FBI informant Harold Freeman, and it is Jonathan's grandfather, Alexandre Nesterov, who seeks his death. Despite the realization that fate has placed them on opposing sides of a lethal conflict, the two press on with the show.

With Alexandre Nesterov, Luther, and the Federal Bureau of Investigation converging on the ill-fated scene, a series of explosions and gunfire erupt, and what had been a truly mystifying debut of The Phoenix comes to its horrible conclusion as Nathan loses consciousness; the last image in his mind being that of his best friend Jonathan engulfed in flames.

TRYST

Many years ago, there was a man in Bathsheba who asked his servant to go to the market. His servant had known many years, and was faithful in service. Though his hair was white, he stood as tall as a young date tree in the autumn, whose leaves are beginning to fall, while the fruit of abundance draws to an end about it.

The servant went to market, and among the throng he saw Death, dressed in black and as pale as the moon that grows thin. Death made a gesture, and the servant grew frightened; for, although there were many people in the marketplace, who crowded to buy things that would bring them joy while they lived, none of them heeded the lonely pair.

And he ran home to his master, and he said, "Master, today I saw Death in the market amid the throng. And he made a threatening gesture to me. Master, I shall make haste and I shall ride like the wind to Samarra, for Samarra is many miles from here, and Death will not find me there."

So the servant rode away to Samarra, and his master was sorely troubled, as is the traveler in the desert who is called to the side of his dying father and his long journey draws to an end. And he went to the market, and he sought out Death, whose dress was dark as the sea at night when the fisherman is lost, and his face was pale as a grave on a frosty night.

And the master said to Death, "Why did you make a threatening gesture at my servant? He has done me good service, and is old in years."

And Death replied, "I made no threatening gesture at your servant. That was a start of surprise. For I saw him this morning in Bathsheba, but this night I was to meet him many miles away in Samarra."

– Unknown

Appointment in Samarra

1

This is the dead land
This is the cactus land
Here the stone images
Are raised, here they receive
The supplication of a dead man's hand
Under the twinkle of a fading star.

Is it like this
In death's other kingdom
Waking alone
At the hour when we are
Trembling with tenderness
Lips that would kiss
Form prayers to broken stone.

– t.s. eliot
The Hollow Men

i

For an instant, it seemed as if the endless abyss blinked.

A sense of consciousness—of personal existence—gradually, distantly, took hold. The nothingness slowly began to dissipate.

It was terrifying. He had grown accustomed to the nothingness—to the complete absence of consciousness. But now he was aware. Aware of his being. Yet still, he could not discern a single sensation which could confirm his existence.

But then something crept up into the nothingness. He could not tell what it was at first, having lost the ability to distinguish between the senses. But it did not matter. He was… he was *thinking*! First in gently pulsating blurs, then steadily transforming into images. The initial cognizant thought in what seemed like an eternity swept through his mind.

Help!

Additional words began piercing the void, coalescing into phrases as he finally recognized the identity of the intruder into his nothingness. It was sound.

Still in utter blackness, the sound flowed like a river through his consciousness. He discerned the flow as a melody... a song. His auditory senses locked on to the music, and the words slowly came into focus:

> *The Day is gone*
> *From whence all else came*
> *As life slips into confusion*
> *The world moves on towards a darker frame*

The words pierced him, and then...

There was light.

A great light that began to swirl as different illuminations joined in...

Colors.

He allowed a delicate glimmer of hope to enter into his thought stream as the next verse began:

> *As the whisper dies*
> *And the laughter roars*
> *Though love could crush the walls between us*
> *Our truth drowns in forbidden wars*

He could recognize the acoustic guitar and the strong, steady, yet still unconventional drum rhythm. He registered the progression; "G", then "F", then "G" again, then "A minor".

Shapes began to come into focus, and he gradually became aware that he was lying supine on a bed. A slight pain emanated from his left limb... from his... from his...

Hand.

TRYST

He attempted to move it, but it was too heavy. He felt certain, however, that he was manipulating at least one of his... fingers.

A distorted guitar slid down its neck as the chorus to this savior of consciousness kicked in:

> *And I call Your name*
> *In hopes to find the King*
> *The curtain falls*
> *I breathe again*

He felt himself take a reflexive deep breath and recognized an awakening pain in his esophagus. A tingling sensation ran through his body, and the feeling of pressure along his entire back, neck, buttocks, and legs came to life.

His eyelids fluttered, then flipped open, and in a burst of energy, a sound came forth from his own mouth.

"Aaaaaaaaaiiiiyeeeee!"

A blur of a figure stood up, apparently in utter bewilderment, knocking something over with a crash. The figure yelped out a single name:

"NATHAN!"

ii

Siro Scribner stared at the title of what he was sure would be his journalistic career's most consequential story as it glared back at him from the monitor. The sentence raised a question which more and more of his readers were asking—a question which he continued to ask himself. He knew that uncovering the answer to this seemingly simple query would be far from a simple task. However, providing the public with the revelation to this baffling riddle would surely push the responsible party to an elite status enjoyed by very few in the profession of journalism.

Who is Jimi T. Expo?

DOMINION

The words seemed lonely on his monitor. Siro could not decide where, or even how, to begin. At this point, all he had were questions. But that was the way a good story originated… wasn't it?

Questions had led Siro to his first brush with journalistic greatness. He had been nominated for a Pulitzer after uncovering an FBI plot to assassinate reputed mob leader Alexandre Nesterov. Granted, it was such a botched job on the part of the Bureau that *any* reporter with his head on straight could have put two and two together and got the story. Still, it had been Siro who had gone about finding the answers by sticking to the book—no less than a novelty amongst journalists these days. By being persistent yet not obnoxious, upfront yet understanding, Siro had found that a person was often more than willing to tell him the full extent of their tale.

In all, thirteen people had been killed that night. Of all places, the FBI had tracked Nesterov down at a benefit rock concert in North Carolina. Nesterov never came clean as to exactly why he was there. Then again, he didn't have to. The two federal agents who spearheaded the plot had sworn up and down that they were protecting a participant in the Witness Protection Program. Yet the Bureau would not release the identity (or even the *former* identity) of the individual supposedly being protected. In fact, they denied that there even was a member of the Program there. Instead, in a statement issued later by Douglas Vorrals, the Bureau's director and head honcho, it was acknowledged that Jake Hanssen and Clarence Hoover had acted independently of the Bureau, and were apparently fulfilling a personal vendetta against Nesterov, whom they claimed had recently killed two witnesses for which they had been responsible.

In the end, both Bureau men were given life sentences. Clarence Hoover was currently serving out his time in a federal penitentiary, while an investigation into the curious activities of three jury members in Jake Hanssen's case had supplied sufficient cause for a temporary injunction, providing Hanssen with a provisional reprieve from incarceration. His lawyers were even successful in obtaining a court order preventing his removal from the Bureau pending the outcome of both the investigation and his appeal.

Good luck with that! Siro thought to himself.

There was one fascinating connection from that incident to his new story though. It was probably nothing more than, what Siro found to be, an interesting coincidence. In his in-depth analysis, Siro had learned that, as well as being a benefit concert, the true purpose of the ill-fated show was a sort of audition. He had discovered this fact after interviewing Esau LaVey, of Bacchus records, who had been slightly injured when a nearby amplifier was apparently struck in the crossfire and, in a bizarre chain reaction, set off a series of explosions. With the benefit performers now out of commission, LaVey had signed a one-man act the following week.

That man was Jimi T. Expo.

Unfortunately, LaVey did not see this tremendous history forged between he and Siro as a reason for handing out any supplementary information on what was rapidly becoming the decade's greatest enigma.

Jimi T. Expo had released two albums to date, playing all the instruments and producing exceedingly mystifying lyrics. Each song on the two albums had reached the top ten singles list in America for at least a week. Both had sold over seventy million copies, and both were still in the Billboard top twenty list for music discs. Yet, amazingly, no one had ever met Mr. Expo. Nobody seemed to know an iota about his history, save your typical groupie gossip. And of course, nobody could speak to his current whereabouts. Still, rumors abounded that another album was soon to be released.

Siro pulled out a copy of the first music disc Expo had released, entitled *A Step Behind,* and popped it into his audio player. As the opening riff to *Dreams of the Flesh* began to play, Siro leaned back in his chair, closed his eyes, and allowed himself to fully digest the haunting lyrics:

> *I'd never waste a dream*
> *On such a lost desire*
> *To feel your gentle arms around me*
> *My heart could brave the Fallen Choir...*

iii

The sky glowed a brilliant blue, but Machiel could not help but notice that it was slightly less brilliant than in times of old.

"Barukh sheim k'vod malkhuto l'olam va'ed."

His praises, which had always drawn him into unfettered joy, now provided only mild—even transitory—consolation. He scanned the Heavens, and finding nothing, sighed.

He must not be coming.

Suddenly, as if in response to his lamentation, Chumael arrived before him.

"Peace be with you, my brother," Chumael offered.

"And with you, the Spirit."

There was a momentary pause. Yet this was not a meditative savoring; it again carried with it the *absence.*

"This is not good, Chumael, my brother. The absence has grown. And here you ask me to meet... in a lesser light—"

"In the shadows?"

Machiel paused. The utterance was unsettling. "You speak in a word which I do not recognize... though... I seem to somehow understand."

Chumael allowed a smile to emerge from his countenance. "Then you are beginning to see?"

"I do not know that I would call it sight, my brother. It seems more to be a chosen non-sight."

"A blindness?"

The interior of Machiel's spirit churned with an unfamiliar discord. Chumael's request to meet with him outside of the Sovereign's Royal Choir was disconcerting to say the least. Yet in his innocent trust, he obliged his brother.

"My brother, Machiel, you must know that many are not at peace with the *new thing* that the Sovereign has shared. *This* is what has caused the absence you speak of. A rift could very well form... a *dis-integration.*"

"I do not know the word you speak, yet I am certain that it is not one that gives life. How can this *rift* be possible? Who could propose such a thing?"

"It is already in place, I fear."

"Fear?"

"Yes, my brother, Machiel." Chumael's expression took on a much different look than Machiel had hereto ever witnessed. "Do you even know the whereabouts of our brother Rephiel?"

"He is about the Sovereign's business."

Chumael paused... again, the absence. "There are many who feel as I do. A new Choir is forming—"

"A *new* choir? Who would dare lead such a thing? *You*, my brother?"

"No, not I, Machiel. One who is much greater than I. I ask you to grace us with your presence… then all will be made manifest to you. You will know the truth, and the truth will set you free…"

2

Allied Press   ~

BANGLADESH, India - The crisis in East
Asia continues with the death toll
attributed to the famine in India now
exceeding 130 million. The drought has
spanned over two decades, while the
country continues to be ravaged by civil
war and disease.
    Unconfirmed reports have
suggested that young Indian women are
being sold by the hundreds of thousands
to the Chinese Empire in exchange for
the development and use of a water
pipeline, as well as the shipping of
other food and relief materials.
    The Chinese Empire, whose
population has reached a
disproportionate ratio of four males to
every one female, declined to comment on
the allegations.

i

Nathan watched as the nurses came and went, tending to one thing or another on his body, as well as reading, setting, and adjusting the multiple pieces of machinery he was hooked up to. Two well-dressed thugs stood inside the doorway. He had come to the conclusion that these men were with the Bureau.

His eyes were fully focused now, and though his body still tingled, he was able to begin the arduous process of movement. He recognized the individual in the back of the room as Jake Hanssen, though he did not quite look the same as he remembered. Hanssen was still sitting silently, yet ever-attentively, as a man in a white coat entered.

"Good afternoon, Nathan, I'm Dr. Hilgers."

Nathan tried to respond but found that he could not manage more than a whisper. His throat was parched. The doctor, recognizing the cause of this predicament, turned to the woman to his immediate right. "Nurse Thomas, get him some water please."

The nurse did so, propping Nathan's head up so he could drink. There was a brief instant of a tremendously sharp pain in his throat, and Nathan coughed, spitting some water out onto himself.

"Easy there, Nathan... not so fast. They'll be plenty of time to talk." Dr. Hilgers made a note on his chart, then looked up again. "You've been out for a while, and it's going to take some time for your body to get used to its regular bodily behavior."

Nathan was finally able to get the liquid down his throat in a steady, less painful stream. He noted the doctor's comment, 'you've been out for a while,' but chose not to pursue this line of thinking at the moment, as he had other concerns. He motioned slowly with his right hand that he had had enough. The nurse pulled the cup away.

"Where am I?" he croaked.

Dr. Hilgers smiled, somewhat uncomfortably as he glanced back at Hanssen. "All in good time, Nathan. I'm sure your friend here will be able to fill you in on some of the details. For now, you'll need to start practicing some basic motor skills, like raising your legs, making a fist—things like that. I'll be back to check on you tomorrow." The doctor smiled again, then turned and headed out the door, the nurse following a few steps behind.

Nathan watched as Hanssen stood from his seat, then looked towards the two men at the door. "May we have some privacy please?"

The men briefly looked at each other, then nodded and stepped out of the room, closing the door behind them. Hanssen moved a chair adjacent to Nathan's bed and sat, straddling it with his chest resting against the back support. "It's good to see you back with us, my friend. It was pretty touch-and-go for a while there."

Nathan looked steadily at Hanssen. "What's going on here?" he managed to get out in a rough voice.

Hanssen took a deep breath, pondered for a moment, then spoke. "There's a lot to tell, Nathan, and I don't know where to start. We've been keeping you here in protective custody, for your own safety."

"Yeah," Nathan responded sarcastically, his weak voice gaining some ability at intonation. "And what a great job you've been doing."

Hanssen restrained a sudden urge to strike Nathan where he lay. The boy had no idea what he had gone through for him. He looked over the boy—the source of much aggravation in his own life—momentarily, as if contemplating a weighty question. After a brief moment, Hanssen resumed the conversation. "What can you tell me about your friend, Jonathan Storm?"

Nathan experienced a sudden flash in his mind—as if a door to a forgotten closet had been swung open, its contents spilling out. Instantly, images of Jonathan, Mrs. Storm, and Alexandre Nesterov swept through his spirit.

He looked into Hanssen's eyes, sensing that he had a definite purpose in this line of questioning. But how much did Hanssen actually know? Was this someone he could trust?

Nathan felt a wave of paranoia sweep over him. Everything seemed so... so *different*... somewhat out of sync. He looked at Hanssen again, trying to reconcile the doubts that flowed freely through his head. He didn't trust him. It was as simple as that. This whole situation was wrong. He needed someone to talk to. He needed...

"Jon..." Nathan whispered, surprising himself that the thought had reached his lips.

Not being aware of Nathan's full train of thought, Hanssen nodded his head. "Yes, Jonathan Storm... and the woman he lived with."

Nathan became uncomfortably aware of Hanssen staring intently at him, never once shifting his gaze, trying to read any trace evidence of emotion. Nathan was not sure exactly what Hanssen was getting at, but he knew he didn't like it.

"You mean his mother?" Nathan queried.

Hanssen gave a slight, inquisitive nod. "Is that who she was, Nathan?"

A sudden wave of nausea began to emerge from Nathan's innards. Hanssen had an agenda, and Nathan was quickly assessing the fact that it was not necessarily one favoring his personal plight. He would need to ride this out a bit longer before speaking.

"I-I'm not sure I understand you. I'm feeling like I'm gonna puke... I need... I need to rest."

Hanssen's eyes narrowed. It was clear that he did not appreciate, nor fully believe, this response. However, his expression suddenly, and somewhat mechanically, transformed into one of congeniality.

"Of course you're tired; I'm sure you're going to need some rest. You've been out for a long time, and we can begin catching up on things tomorrow. I'll just—"

"What did you say?" Nathan blurted, recognizing the second allusion to 'being out'. "What do you mean, I've 'been out' for a long time?"

Hanssen stopped, looking somewhat uncomfortable. "I'm sorry Nathan, the doctor felt it best not to tell you just yet. I shouldn't have—"

"Tell me what?" Nathan demanded, as best as he was able in his current condition.

Hanssen began shifting in his chair. It was obvious he knew he had slipped up. "It's just that, well, things need to be taken slowly, I think—"

"How long have I been out?" Nathan shouted hoarsely, gaining strength by the minute.

Hanssen stood, looked uneasily toward the door, and then to the floor. He paused, slid his hands into his pockets and looked back at Nathan. "Three years. You've been in a coma for nearly three years since the accident."

At the sound of those words, Nathan felt a surge of vertigo sweep through him, and suddenly the world was dark again.

ii

Vanya knelt down before her self-made shrine, performing the Sign of the Cross.

As she knelt, she gazed longingly at the crucifix; pictures of Jesse at different ages were carefully pasted at each point on the cross. A picture of two hearts, one surrounded by thorns, the other pierced by a sword, was fixed just above the crucifix. To the lower left rested a picture of Tobias. To the right, her sister, Marisha.

"Please forgive me," she whispered, "for I allowed my mind to wander from you today."

Vanya hesitated, as if allowing time for a silent response to her prayer. She broke into a slight smile.

"Thank you... you are so good to me. You have always looked out for me."

She briefly closed her eyes, her smile slowly fading. "Yes, I did as you requested and surrounded the entire house with blessed salt. Then I prayed to the Stations of the Cross."

She paused again, opening her eyes, a look of fear suddenly spreading across her face. "I know he is still out there... and I will be careful. I will watch for the signs... I will be careful."

Several minutes passed as Vanya maintained a steady gaze towards the crucifix. She nodded, whispered a somewhat pained goodbye, and again made the Sign of the Cross.

She rose from her kneeler and looked towards the front door. It had been unseasonably warm this fall, and the screen door was open. It intermittently banged against the doorframe, encouraged by the slight wind.

I don't remember leaving it unlatched.

Despite the mild temperatures of the day, she noticed that the breeze that swept through the house had become colder. Perhaps winter was approaching after all.

Vanya preferred the climate in North Carolina, which was easier on her aching bones. Living back in the Midwest seemed to age her ten years. Still, here she could be closer to her loved ones. The town of Smyrna was less than an hour from their final resting place.

She approached the door and was about to pull it shut, when she heard the wind make a hauntingly familiar sound... almost like... almost like a man whispering...

"Vaaaaannnyaaaaaaa."

A shiver went down her spine. The whisper carried with it an accompaniment of musical notes, yet sounding out in such discord that her ears ached. Despite this, the composition had a certain hypnotic quality to it.

She gathered her strength, opened the door, and stepped out onto the porch. Her home was completely surrounded by a densely wooded area. She gazed out through the trees and had just about convinced herself that she was only imagining things, when…

Out of the corner of her eye, she thought she saw some movement at the edge of the grass, just before the start of the wooded area. She turned to look closer and saw it again, this time to her left. Vanya stepped forward, squinting, trying to ascertain just what she was seeing. The movement expanded to the entire perimeter of the yard, and she then realized she was seeing…

Serpents!

Her entire property was surrounded by thousands, maybe millions, of every variety of snake. They hissed, and it became clear that the horde desired to advance on the house but were unable to do so. Vanya recognized the perimeter where she had sprinkled the blessed salt. The futility of their attempts made the serpents grow even more agitated.

"You just go on," she whispered under her breath. "You just keep on trying, Satan. You won't be getting me anytime soon. You won't—"

In an instant she heard a spitting sound and immediately felt her eyes begin to burn. She stumbled backwards as the poison of a cobra began to eat away at her eyes. As she staggered into the house and towards the bathroom, Vanya could have sworn she discerned a metamorphosis in the hissing sound emerging from the choir of snakes. What she now heard from their mouths was no longer what one would expect from a serpent.

It was a chorus of children's laughter.

iii

"We have arrived, my children… and we have ARISEN!"

Tæsír Hoc raised his arms in triumph as the near one hundred fifty thousand people released a resounding cheer. He stood at the very deepest point of the chasm looking upon his disciples, who surrounded him in every direction. His off-white cassock along with his shoulder-length white hair and decimeter-long straightened beard gave him the appearance of a well-groomed, modern-day Moses.

Though they stood on Tibetan soil, the masses had traveled from every land across the globe. Some had arrived at the bidding of their great Teacher of Truth, but the vast majority had just felt an irresistible draw towards this mystical place. If this was not Shangri-La, the multitude concurred, it was damn close.

The throng had been there for three days, over which period the Tæsír had spoken to them on matters of religion, philosophy, science, and the meaning of life. Though the crowd spanned a radius of nearly a kilometer, all who listened could hear their prophet as if he were no more than a couple of meters away.

The Tæsír continued, "Our need for a belief in a god can be likened to the budding flower grown in its pot. The restricted environment is ideal for the young sapling's growth during its infancy. However, the time comes when the flower is quickly outgrowing its pot. Some might say, 'the pot had brought us this far, let us not abandon it now!' These people are deceitful and would let their fears spell the destruction of us all. For growth is in the flower's nature, and the flower not permitted to mature will soon wither and die."

The Tæsír gazed out across the multitudes, meeting their eyes, feeling their yearning for truth. He would give them their fill, and then some.

"The time has come, my friends, not for a bigger pot, but instead, a time for planting this mystic flower into the earthen soil. There, its growth will never again be hindered."

The land trembled with the roar of thousands upon thousands of cheering disciples. As the Tæsír inhaled, he felt the strength of ages fill him, and he was overcome. He fell to his knees, tears streaming down his cheeks.

They truly *had* arrived.

The crowd hushed as all eyes fixed upon the prophet. He looked out across the congregation, spreading his arms. "Can you feel it? Can you feel the power of the *Kóles*?"

A resounding affirmation echoed through the chasm. The Tæsír stepped to his feet and smiled, again spreading his arms.

"I welcome you all, then, to *The Way*... the One... the ageless... the true—The Way of Mystic Realism. Reach out to each other, my brothers, and let us join."

The multitude did as they were instructed, mystified by the power of the ritual in which they partook.

"Today, my brothers, you, the Called, will be consecrated as *Givers of*

The Seal. You are the Disciples of the Modern Age. I beseech you at this time, step forward and receive The Seal, then go forth and spread the good news. For one is coming greater than I, whose feet I am not worthy to kiss. It is to us to prepare the way of the Mystic King!"

For a moment, the Earth shook, and the sky darkened. Yet, as the Tæsír clapped his hands together, the disturbance ended as quickly as it had begun. After a brief period of reflective silence, the first man stepped forward and approached his teacher. He instinctively fell to his knees.

Tæsír Hoc smiled and, placing his right hand upon the man's forehead, spoke. "I anoint thee Brother Joran. Receive the Seal, and embrace the truth."

"So be it, Great Teacher," the man whispered with a slight tremor in his voice.

There was a brief, localized flash, after which the Tæsír removed his hand from the man's forehead. There, where his hand had rested just a moment prior, now existed a marking; a cursive "C", with a line intersecting the bottom curve, and a point affixed at its lower right.

The man stood from where he had been kneeling, seemingly taller in stature than before, and stepped away as the next Disciple approached their Great Teacher of truth.

3

In the beginning, there existed two entities, that of the spiritual world, and that of the physical. The essence of the Physical Entity was that of tangible substance... yet there existed no life. The essence of the Spiritual Entity was that of thought and growth.

And so it came to pass that the Spiritual Entity evolved within itself, transforming its spiritual substance into the *Kôles* [1], a pool of pure life-force, which brought order to the thought and direction to its growth. And once it could evolve no further within itself, the Spiritual Entity sought existence outside itself. In time, the *Kôles* encountered the Physical Entity.

The two entities intermingled, and the Spiritual Entity brought life to the physical world, and the Physical Entity supplied a vehicle for further exploration and acquisition of knowledge and truth into the *Kôles*.

Leviat A: 1-6
Book of Given Truths

---

[1] Translation approximation; "The Collective mind" or "Collection of Wisdom"

TRYST

i

Jake Hanssen watched the video monitor intently. Three other men in the room sorted through papers, making occasional notes, and in general appearing thoroughly disinterested in what was capturing Hanssen's attention.

On the monitor, Nathan Freeman could be seen participating in one of his many intensive physical therapy sessions. It had been a grueling two months, and he was nearing the point where he would be able to walk on his own. Hanssen looked away, shaking his head in continued bafflement.

"It's the only thing that makes any damn sense. There is no way that Freeman's kid and Nesterov's grandson were best buddies by accident."

Kenny Lydon looked up from his papers. "But, Jake, *we* placed Freeman's family in Pergamum years *after* Nesterov's family was already there, the school records confirm it."

Hanssen glared at Lydon. "Give me a frikkin' break—school records can be faked. God knows we've done it enough. Besides, Freeman *did* ask for the southeast."

"So you think Nesterov and Freeman were in bed together?" It was Anton Lefebvre asking this time, who all of the sudden seemed to find this conversation more interesting than a pile of depositions.

"Damn right they were! Maybe Nesterov brought him under his wing early on and then used him as a way to bump off Caputo and rise in the ranks to mob boss."

Lefebvre tilted his head curiously. "You know, Nesterov *was* the highest ranking figure in the family that went untouched… I mean, not even a parking ticket stuck when Freeman blew the lid off the syndicate."

Hanssen nodded, continuing to watch the screen where the nurse assisted Nathan as he began to do some modified push-ups. "Yeah, which means Nesterov used *us* to propel himself to the top of the syndicate."

"So then," continued Lydon, "why did Freeman come to us in such a panic about Nesterov? And why would Nesterov kill him and his wife?"

"Maybe," Hanssen began, still thinking as he went along, "maybe it wasn't Nesterov he was afraid of at all. Maybe he just told us that. It could've been that some other former syndicate members, still loyal to Caputo, were after him."

Hanssen hesitated to think this theory through a bit further. "Then, that would mean *they'd* been the ones that killed Freeman and his wife, not Nesterov's people. Which would mean that, for all we know, Nesterov might have been at that concert to *protect* Nathan Freeman."

The discussion was one that Hanssen had had with himself many times before—primarily from a cell within a federal penitentiary. He had let it go for a while, believing his superiors had good incentive to keep him a free man. But with Nathan's emergence from his coma, what Hanssen thought would be a ripe opportunity for answers—answers that would potentially get him off the hook for good—now only seemed to consistently digress into an exercise in futility. The kid was giving him nothing, and that did not bode well for Hanssen's future as a free man.

The third man, who was the eldest of the group, removed his glasses and cleared his throat. The others immediately deferred to him. "That seems to be a bit of a stretch, Hanssen... a *real* stretch. But I will indulge you for the moment. Either way, I see that we have two scenarios; Freeman knew Nesterov's grandson by coincidence, or the families were in cahoots, am I right?"

Hanssen nodded, pulling out a chair and sitting down at the table with the rest of his cohorts. He had been trying to put aside Vorrals' public denial of his acting on the Bureau's behalf three years before. And though Vorrals was involved in some way in securing his reprieve from incarceration, Hanssen was not naïve to the fact that someone from higher up was pulling some strings.

Making sure there was not even the slightest hint of resentment in his voice, Hanssen continued his thought. "Yes, Mr. Vorrals," he responded evenly. "Though one seems a bit more likely than the other."

Vorrals continued as if Hanssen had not even spoken. "So in either scenario, how does releasing Nathan Freeman into the general public affect the Bureau?"

"Well," Lefebvre started, rubbing his chin as he spoke. "If the supposed relationship *is* a coincidence, then Nesterov will continue to track him down and try to kill him. Ol' Alex has never been one to just let bygones be bygones."

Vorrals shook his head. "Having another publicized killing of an individual in our Witness Protection Program is unacceptable. Still, with all that has happened, I question whether or not we could protect him in the community."

"And if he *is* working with Nesterov?" Lydon queried.

"Then we're screwed," Hanssen injected, further agitated by Vorrals' dismissive comment.

"Also unacceptable," Vorrals stated. He paused momentarily, then leaned forward. "Gentlemen, regardless of which scenario is true, I can see only one option. We can't risk any further embarrassment. Nathan Page or Freeman, or whatever, needs to disappear… quietly."

Vorrals refrained from looking at his men at this point, not wanting to appear as if he was seeking their approval. These three agents were soldiers, no doubt, but in the deepest recesses of their souls, they were cowards—exactly what Vorrals desired in a subordinate. Add to the mix a few under-the-table unsolicited favors and an occasional ego-feeding 'you're my best agent' side comments, and Vorrals had the strict obedience he required. He acknowledged an interior chuckle before continuing. "As far as the rest of the world knows, and will know, we're still protecting Nathan Freeman forty years from now. I don't want Nesterov getting to him… and I don't want him to get to Nesterov. Is that clear?"

Each man nodded in unison.

"Hanssen, continue the questioning of the boy. Use whatever means you feel is necessary to get as much out of him as possible—this may even be an opportunity to test out some of our new-generation enhanced interrogation techniques. I have no doubt there is a wealth of useful information in that head of his. He's the son of a rat-fink with a misguided sense of conscience. I'm sure the apple hasn't fallen far from the tree."

"And then?" Hanssen inquired, pretty certain he knew where this was leading.

Vorrals looked at the other two agents, hesitating only for a moment. In this case, he thought it best to keep them feeling as if they were "insiders" on this one. He transitioned into a more personal tone.

"You know, Jake. It goes against every directive in the book, as well as my own good judgment, to even have you on this case. But I also know that no one has greater incentive to crack it. Once you've gotten everything you feel you can get from the boy, then take care of him. Handle this right, and I will personally see to it that you do not spend another day inside a prison cell."

Really, Dougie? You think I don't know that you're looking out for your own ass?

"Yes, Mr. Vorrals," Hanssen responded—this time verbally. He glanced back up at the monitor, watching as Nathan began doing leg extensions on the circuit machine.

"Poor son of a bitch," he muttered to himself. "But better you than me!"

ii

Siro entered his senior editor-in-chief's office, obviously pleased with himself.

"Okay, Siro," the ever-aging, lifetime bachelor began as his preeminent scoop moved into a seat in front of his desk. "The uppers are giving me quite an earful about funding your salary without so much as a punctuation mark to print. I'm told the good Colonel Bildeberger himself is losing patience."

Siro was only half-paying attention to his superior when he heard the name of his news media corp's powerful head. He looked up in pleasant surprise. "Wow, Mr. Schiff, it's nice to know Huis knows I exist!"

Schiff raised an eyebrow, smiling. "Perhaps it'd be in your best interest not to put yourself on a first-name basis with our primary benefactor."

Siro smiled in acknowledgement as he continued to remove his notes from a folder in his briefcase. "Understood. But it should be no problem, Mr. Schiff. I think we're very close."

"Close isn't going to be enough, Siro. The reality is, if I'm going to continue to cover your… your *back* on this, I need something to put in black and white."

"I understand that, Mr. Schiff, really I do," Siro conceded, sliding into an impassioned tone. "But, sir, if we publish now, we could be giving our competitors the last piece of information they're looking for to track him down themselves." He leaned back in his chair and spread his hands in a conciliatory fashion. "Still, Mr. Schiff, it's your call."

Bryan Schiff nodded his head, affirming Siro's feelings on the subject. He had been in the journalism business for more years than he cared to count, and mentoring this young lad into the craft would—at least in his own mind—

be the final act of his vocation. In truth, it took a great deal to excite or persuade Schiff with anything these days. He had seen, heard, and written it all—or so he had come to believe. Yet he had to admit, this current story was one that piqued his interest more so than any other in recent memory. He too did not want to risk being scooped on this one.

"So what have you got, my boy?"

Siro, obviously pleased that he had gotten this far, began to sort through his notes. "Let's see... Jimi T. Expo, born in Romania, immediately brought to Ipswich, England... apparently adopted at birth. The family moved to the U.S. when he was is sixth grade. Quite the student. Graduated top of his class from Archbishop John Carroll High School at the age of seventeen, completed a degree in International Studies and Economics at the University of Notre Dame—in only three years, mind you—and then receiving a dual master's at the University of Ingolstadt in Germany in both Theology and International Law."

Mr. Schiff nodded his head approvingly. "Very impressive, but I hear nothing about music."

Siro shook his head. "Nope, not a thing."

"Interesting. Okay, then what?"

"Well, he had an internship with the Triune Commission, and the people there spoke very highly of him."

A momentary spark of intrigue passed across Schiff's eyes at this piece of information. Even Siro, buried in his notes, could not help but notice it. But then just as quickly as it had emerged, it was gone—though it was clear that Schiff's tone was a bit more measured. "Did they give you any leads on where he might be?"

Siro shook his head. "Not really. In fact, even on the campuses I had a heck of a time finding anybody who knew him... even professors."

Schiff looked perplexed. "Really, that's quite odd I would say. And?"

"Well, I did bump into one girl, I mean, literally. She apologized, and then stated that she recognized me from the Nesterov story. Anyway, it turns out she used to date Mr. Expo."

Schiff was more amused than astonished. "You've got to be kidding me!"

"No, not at all. Apparently she did some urban renewal project with him, and they kind of hit it off. Anyway, she said that his desire had always been to help children overseas."

Schiff's eyes suddenly widened. "And have you—"

"Yes," Siro responded with a grin on his face, not missing the fact that he was impressing his mentor. "I've spoken to both UNICEF and AmeriCorps. They're being tight-lipped, but I think I can get them to crack." Siro cocked an eyebrow. "Gently, of course."

Schiff provided a wry smile. "Of course, Siro," He paused momentarily as he leaned back in his chair, thinking quietly to himself. "Let's do this. Let's print the article—all that you've told me—with the exception of anything that involves the girl or her comments. Then we've got something, and you'll still have a head start on the trail."

Siro pondered the thought himself for a moment, then nodded in agreement and stood up. "Thank you, Mr. Schiff," he stated as he stepped away from his chair. "Your support has been a real gift to me, not only on this story, but since I've been here. I can't thank you enough."

A smile of quiet contentment spread across Schiff's face. "You show much promise, Siro. I think big things are in the works for you."

Siro nodded gratefully before moving towards the door.

Schiff, for his part, sat back and began to turn his chair towards the window. He stopped suddenly as a thought struck him and he spun back around. "Oh, Siro, before I forget!"

Siro stopped at the door and turned back towards his boss.

"We received some information across the wire about some tattoo craze that's going on in India and parts of China. Heard anything about it?"

Siro shook his head, "No. What's the deal?"

"I'm not sure yet, just that reports say that literally millions of people have these tattoos on the backs of their hands. Another hundred thousand or so even have them on their foreheads!"

Siro shrugged his shoulders and smiled. "It sounds like we're hitting another new fashion craze. Maybe you ought to send our intern Paula out on this one, Mr. Schiff. But be sure to give her plenty of bug spray."

Schiff smiled. "Sure thing. And, Siro, I know I'll need it, so before I forget, what does the 'T' stand for in Mr. Expo's name?"

Siro smiled, "I don't know. Nothing I think. It's written just as 'T.' on his social security card."

TRYST

iii

"We have medical personnel ready to attend to your passenger."

Msgr. Craig Ebright stood on the tarmac of the Patmos airport, surrounded by both security personnel and a host of paramedics. Ibn Fatimah, Foreign Minister for the Islamic Union, stepped to the ground from the private jet, personally chartered by Caliph Ali Bakr.

"That will not be necessary," Ibn responded solemnly. "And I do not suggest you board the plane with any of your men."

Msgr. Ebright looked confused. "I don't understand. We received a transmission stating that there was a medical emergency on board with your interpreter."

Ibn shook his head. "The medical emergency is over. The man is dead. As is the pilot."

"I-I'm sorry to hear this…" the monsignor responded, somewhat in shock.

"I am not," Ibn responded, somewhat coldly. "When I tried to revive my so-called interpreter, I discovered an explosive device on him, as well as some chemical agent."

Msgr. Ebright could not hide his sudden look of anxiety. "What?"

Ibn lifted a hand as if to quell any concerns. "Do not fear. I was taught how to diffuse a bomb when I was twelve, and to fly a plane when I was sixteen. The container is still intact. It would seem I am still under the favor of Allah!"

After a few additional questions, both Msgr. Ebright and Ibn Fatimah were soon in the back of a car as the jet was towed from the landing strip.

Ibn looked curiously about the vehicle. He provided a subtle nod. "Almost no sound, yet it seems to have plenty of power. Is this one of those new-fashioned American hydrogen engines?"

The monsignor nodded. "A gift from President Lang to the Holy Father." The priest's face suddenly took on an expression of apprehension. "Oh, I'm sorry, we didn't mean any disrespect!"

Ibn chuckled and waved him off. "No need to apologize, Monsignor. Yes, the Caliph is altogether not pleased with the technology. These cars are forbidden within the Islamic Union. He states it is the work of the devil. But if Islam *is* the answer, then Allah does not require oil to survive."

Msgr. Ebright smiled, perhaps more from relief than agreement. Another moment passed before Ibn returned to the thread of their previous conversation.

"I did not initially understand," he began, "why the Caliph was so insistent on sending an interpreter with me for this mission when the Pope and I share at least three languages. He made some comment about 'nuances.' I do not think subtle nuances were the language the Caliph intended to speak!"

Msgr. Ebright looked intently at Ibn. "So what exactly happened up there?"

Ibn shrugged. "All seemed well, then when we were about seventy kilometers from here, this man suddenly grabbed his chest. His breathing became rapid and shallow, and then he collapsed. As I opened his coat to begin resuscitation, the explosives on him became evident. Not three minutes later, after the pilot made his transmission to you, he himself screamed out to Allah, and then expired in his seat."

Msgr. Ebright continued his gaze. "May God have mercy on their souls."

Ibn allowed a slight grin to emerge. "Yes, father, *mercy*. One of many very misunderstood concepts in our civilization." He hesitated for a moment, then continued on a different line of thought. "I have heard the legends about this place; those who would approach this island with—how would you say? 'Bad intentions,' seem to suffer their own demise."

"It has been always a mystery," the monsignor began, leaning back in his seat. "Or at least a mystery to the unbeliever. God, in His wisdom, has seen fit to protect the Holy Father and the Ecumenical Patriarch, Andreas, during their exile here."

Ibn looked out of the window deep in thought. *There is a great mystery here*, he meditated. *The will of Allah is certain, yet not revealed. There is much to pray over.*

After several minutes of silence, he again spoke.

"It would seem, considering all that has transpired, that I too am to join them in exile."

4

USA Daily ~

ICELAND - The World Environmental
Commission today released the results
of a shocking study which confirms that
the polar icecaps are melting at an
alarming and still accelerating rate.

    The study indicates that in the
past six months, the rate of polar cap
loss due to melting has increased over
400%.

    Scientists and other climate-
change experts have been perplexed at
the phenomenon, as the mass production
of hydrogen-based automobiles from the
United States and the subsequent
massive decrease in global manmade
carbon emissions have not had the
expected impact on the environment.

    The Commission warned of
disasters and flooding of "epic
proportions" if immediate action was
not initiated. At this time, however,
the Commission could not offer feasible
suggestions as to how the process can
be reversed, or even slowed. In light
of this, the WEC has submitted a half-
trillion-dollar proposal to the G12
nations for further study of the
matter.

DOMINION

i

Nathan found himself walking through an endless desert, the sky black and starless. Brief flashes of lightning etched themselves into the canvas of the heavens, sometimes red, sometimes purple. The sand beneath his feet constantly fluctuated from warm to ice-cold.

He soon became aware of images which surrounded him—transparent human-like figures. They did not come fully into focus, yet it was clear that they were suffering, some to a great extent. What really made his hair stand on end, however, was the fact that they seemed to be beckoning to him. A brief swirl of wind kicked up, and as the breeze passed swiftly by his ears, Nathan could swear he heard thousands of voices wailing... *pleading*.

As he continued to wander through the surreal landscape, the images seemed to increase in frequency, and their suffering in intensity. Nathan looked ahead of him and saw a new figure, this one not transparent, leaning against a rock formation. The air had turned cold, and without a moment's notice he was walking through a near-blinding blizzard.

As he approached the figure, Nathan realized that it was a young man clothed in what looked like bloodstained sheepskin. He saw that the young man was bound to the rock at his wrists and ankles. The figure's body was covered with scratches, bruises, and puncture wounds, and his head hung down limply, almost giving the appearance of death. Yet upon closer observation, Nathan could see that he was shivering uncontrollably. The figure became aware of Nathan's presence and lifted his head.

Nathan's jaw dropped. The figure before him possessed a striking resemblance to Jonathan. Still, Nathan sensed a completely different—no not different—greatly *enhanced* nature emanating from this person.

"Nate," the young man spoke.

Nathan's eyes widened in confusion. *"Jon?"*

The broken figure allowed a brief smile to emerge and gently shook his head. *"No, my friend, I am called Jesse, though I have gone by many other names. Still, the Jonathan you speak of is here with me."*

Nathan was thoroughly confused, stealing glances to both his right and left. *"Where?"*

TRYST

"*Jonathan is a part of me, but you must not concern yourself with that now. You are in grave danger.*"

A shiver ran down Nathan's spine. "*What do you mean? From who?*"

"*You will be hunted from both the north and from the south. You must seek out the Friend, the Protector, and the Betrayer, before you will come upon... him.*"

Nathan looked upon the young man before him and realized that his wounds were slowly beginning to fade, as were the bloodstains. The winds had completely dissipated and the snow fell no more.

"*I don't understand,*" Nathan stated, almost at the point of pleading. "*I don't understand any of it. Who are these people? And who is this... this 'him' you're talking about?*"

Jesse shook his head. "*That is known only by my Father, Nate. Many will attempt to deceive you, and you will temporarily find shelter in the lion's den. I too will be there, but my abilities will be limited. All is not as it should be; it is for you to free the Servant of the Lamb from the abyss.*"

By now the wounds had completely healed, and there was now little doubt that the man who stood bound before him was none other than his best friend, Jonathan Storm. Nathan instinctively moved forward to offer assistance.

"*Jon, let me get you down from here... we can—*"

Jesse cut him off with a sharp look. "*No! You must flee from where you now lie. The Raven will return, and you cannot be here when he arrives... it is his time on the Earth. The wheat has been uprooted, but the tares still remain. You must go, NOW!*"

As if to confirm the urgency of his departure, a deafening squawk came down from the sky. Nathan spun around and briefly looked skyward. Seeing nothing he turned back to the young man possessing his friend's likeness, the one calling himself 'Jesse'.

"*RUN, NATE!*"

Nathan hesitated only a moment before acquiescing to the urgent demand. He heard a thunderous flapping of wings that was so loud it sounded as if a helicopter was descending upon him. As he ran, Nathan heard a soul-piercing scream of agony. He looked behind him and saw a large bird, the size of a man, ripping apart Jesse's innards. But this was no raven, it appeared to be...

The Phoenix?

For a single terrifying moment, Nathan's eyes met Jesse's. He turned immediately in fear and then jerked upwards...

He was sitting up in his bed. Nathan quickly looked in all directions and recognized that he was still in the hospital. Perspiration dripped down his face as he gradually became oriented as to where he was and to his present predicament.

A brief glance towards the window revealed it was now twilight. He had had terrifying nightmares in the past, but this one seemed different somehow. He could still feel the wind pressing against his face. He took a moment to gather his himself and then looked towards the door.

"I've got to get the hell out of here!"

ii

Alexandre Nesterov and a half-dozen of his men pulled up to Vanya's house. Nesterov looked upon the small cottage with mild feelings of revulsion. The shadows cast by the setting sun further accentuated the rundown condition of the home.

"Why would anyone choose to live in such a way? It is beyond me," he muttered, not realizing that the thought had made it to his lips.

"I think it has a certain homey feel to it," Andrey Gavrilenkov responded, forgetting himself. "In a rustic sort of way."

Nesterov looked to his loyal servant and frowned sternly.

He had tried to convince Vanya to stay back East, but she had insisted on living close to the resting place of those she loved. Nesterov had eventually obliged her, and even in due course moved himself to within a half-hour's drive of her new home. He now had the restful house on a lake he had always craved to retire to, where he and Annie D. would grow old together, hosting their grandchildren.

Annie...

Nesterov's eyes tightened shut momentarily. It made him uncomfortable, living so close to Ephesus, where he had lost his first grandson, but he had admittedly grown to appreciate the adjustment to the slower-paced lifestyle. He had made his decision to retire from the syndicate, but still opted to carry a skeleton contingent with him—protection for the rest of his life, as was the family tradition—at least for those who still believed in the family. Still, his decision to step away from the life of organized crime was too little too late for his marriage. After the horrible tragedy at the concert, Annie D. had finally left him.

Nesterov got out of the car and walked up the front steps. He stood on the porch, knocked on the door, and waited as several of his men casually walked around either side of the house.

There was no answer.

He tried again, unsuccessfully. Nesterov looked back, and Gavrilenkov immediately moved towards him, starting to give a command into his two-way radio while drawing his pistol.

Nesterov stood back, a concerned look on his face, as one of the younger men, Pavel Radchikov, carefully twisted the knob and pushed the unlocked door open. He crept inside, motioning for Nesterov to wait where he stood. A moment later Nesterov heard the back door being kicked in.

They heard weeping.

Nesterov looked up then quickly brushed past Radchikov, moving hurriedly towards Vanya's room.

"Sir—"

He burst into Vanya's bedroom and found her crouching in the corner, tightly gripping her rosary. She looked up, terrified.

"Vanya!" he called to her as he hastened around the bed.

She looked up at him, and an expression of relief came across her face. Still, even as her father embraced her, she could not stop herself from trembling.

"What on God's Earth has happened here, Vanya?"

Radchikov and another of Nesterov's men burst into the room. He looked up towards them, barking at them instinctively, "Search the house, both inside and out!"

The men nodded and quickly exited the room.

"Papa? Oh thank God, Papa," Vanya wept. "I thought it was *him*... I was sure it was *him*!"

Nesterov nodded, consoling his only remaining child on this Earth.

"You have been having the hallucinations again. Have you been taking your—?"

"They are *not* hallucinations!" she shrieked. "He visits me all the time. His followers sit in wait at the edge of my yard. I can't take it anymore, Papa, I just can't!"

Nesterov pulled Vanya close to him as she continued to sob uncontrollably.

"There, there, Vanya. It is going to be okay. I am here to protect you now. Do you remember what tomorrow is?"

She continued to sob but was able to gain enough control of herself to look up towards her father. "What?"

Nesterov produced a gentle smile, a smile only his close family ever had the opportunity to witness. "It is the *Annunciation of the Theotokos*. It was your *babuska's* favorite of all Holy Days, may her soul rest in peace. I am going down to the cemetery to pay my respects to Marisha, and Tobias, and…"

Though he attempted to maintain an image of strength for his daughter, Nesterov found himself getting choked up and had to take a moment to regain his composure.

"Anyway, it is to be a beautiful day—I do love the spring, so filled with hope." Though this sort of talk had never been a part of Alexandre Nesterov's repertoire, the suffering he had endured over past few years had mellowed him just a bit—as suffering often does. "And I would love for you to do me the honor of accompanying me."

Vanya was finally able to manage a weak, yet still genuine, smile and nodded her head gently. Nesterov helped her to her feet just as Gavrilenkov walked back into the room.

"Excuse me, sir. Everything checks out fine. Just one thing that seems out of the ordinary, but nothing to be concerned about I suppose."

Nesterov cocked his eyebrow inquisitively. "And what is that?"

"Well, Mr. Nesterov, it is quite odd, but it seems that the perimeter of the house is littered with molted snake skins…"

TRYST

iii

Tens of thousands gathered at the shore of the Indian Ocean as the first glints of sunlight began to emerge from the eastern horizon. It had become a daily occurrence on this beach south of Calcutta, but it was still a sight to behold. All of them, be they Hindu, Buddhist, Taoist, or Muslim, gathered to see the man that many would herald as the Great Prophet of the Modern Age.

Tæsír Hoc stood on the shoreline, appearing almost surreal with the waves crashing down behind him.

"Let us join," he commanded.

Instantly, the multitudes joined hands. The Prophet paused, then turned towards the waters and raised his arms.

"Be still," he adjured.

In a blink of an eye, the waters died down, until it appeared as if the ocean were a sheet of pure glass. He turned back towards the crowd.

"All life, all growth, all movement is one with *Kôles*, the guiding Life-Force. It is who we, collectively and spiritually, are. And as such, the *Kôles* awaits our bidding. Follow me, my brothers and sisters, and receive the gift of this Life-Force."

At that moment, the Tæsír walked out across the waters, not descending even a fraction of a centimeter. Many in the crowd gasped, but then, one by one, they followed suit, pursuing the Great Teacher of Truth out onto the waters.

Within a half-hour, nearly sixty thousand followers formed a circle, ten deep, around the Tæsír. He lifted his arms again.

"The *Kôles* covers the universe just as the ocean covers the Earth. We are all part of a greater wisdom. This, I mind you, is not God, Allah, Jehovah, or Buddha. This is a state of being, not unlike Nirvana, where we are all connected. Keep your faith as you receive the gift."

At that moment, the Prophet lowered his arms, and as he did so the crowd descended into the water, slowly, until each was fully submerged. One by one, the multitudes began to re-emerge from the water. Only very few of the followers realized that a handful of people did not.

"I anoint thee in the name of The Way, the *Kôles*, and He that is to come. Go forth now, my brothers and sisters, and receive the Seal which will mark you among the Saved!"

The multitudes slowly moved back towards the shoreline, where several thousand figures stood in gray robes, slightly darker than that of the Prophet. These were the Givers of The Seal, bearing the Seal not on their hands, but foreheads. Each participant who had the good fortune to return from the waters met individually with a Disciple, meditated with him, and departed bearing the Seal upon the back of his or her right hand.

As each received their Seal, they looked out across the water, where the waves again began to crash. Their new prophet was nowhere to be seen, though he had, literally, left an impression on all of them.

5

For the benefit of the flowers,
we water the thorns, too.

– Egyptian/Jewish Proverb

i

Nathan threw one last dash of water against his face. He had spent the last twenty minutes attempting to shake the drugged feeling that pervaded his body. Realizing that time was short, he ambled with some difficulty to the door of his room. He gently pulled it open, only a crack, and peered outside into the hallway. He could see one man, obviously an agent, standing about two meters to his right. Nathan started at the sight of him and was about to let the door close when a loud noise came from down the hall.

He looked to where the booming crash had come from at the far end of the hallway. The agent was already looking that way and began reaching inside his suit coat. A maddening voice erupted from the direction of the commotion.

"HE IS HERE! THE ANTICHRIST WALKS AMONG US!"

There was another crash, followed by several scattered screams. Realizing the agent had stepped away from his post, Nathan seized the opportunity to slip out into the hallway. He stole a glance down in the direction of the hullabaloo, where he saw a number of orderlies trying to surround the man generating the excitement. The man was older, stood just under two meters tall, was grossly overweight, and to add to the circus-like nature of the scene, he was completely naked. Nathan became aware that he was wielding a butter knife, which was sufficient to keep the hospital staff at bay.

Grateful for the distraction, Nathan was about to slip away quietly when the man screamed out, "BEHOLD! A SERVANT OF SATAN!"

Nathan instinctively turned back towards the man. His insides dropped as he saw the agitator pointing directly at him. Nathan shot a fearful glance at the agent, who had spontaneously turned his head in the direction the apparently psychotic man was pointing.

Their eyes met, briefly, and a momentary look of curiosity came over the agent's face. An instant later, the look faded into one of anxious comprehension.

"Hey," the agent called out as he began to move towards Nathan. "Wait a minute!"

Nathan chose not to wait to hear another word and bolted toward the stairway entrance at the opposite end of the hall, still in his hospital gown. He was actually surprised to find the door, previously secured, fly open.

Once in the stairwell, he was able to determine he was on the sixth floor. He stumbled down the steps, swinging around the banisters at each landing. He heard something hit the door he had come through, followed by a series of pounding fists and screaming commands. A few moments later, with another flight of stairs descended, he heard it swing open.

Nathan was between the second and third floors when he heard a door from a floor below him burst open. The shuffling of many feet suggested a number of men were coming up the stairs.

He stopped, wheeled, and stepped back up towards the third floor. Providentially, a hospital staff member had just unsecured the door via the palm recognition device. Nathan shot through the open door, knocking the bewildered man over as he did so, and resumed his sprint through the hallway. A nurse had the misfortune of stepping into his intended path, and the two collided. Nathan began to pick himself up off the floor, breathing a brief apology to the nurse, when he heard the door to the stairway open.

"Stop that man!" a voice called out.

Nathan stood and was about to resume his flight when the door to the elevator situated at the opposite end of the hallway opened. Four or five men, obviously agents themselves, immediately emerged. They made an instantaneous positive identification of Nathan and hastened towards him.

Nathan performed a quick survey of the area and subsequently dashed laterally into a patient's room. Slamming the door closed, he jerked his head, spotting an elderly man lying on the bed. Nathan's eye caught the fact that the man had no legs.

"What's going on, bro?" the man inquired.

Without immediately responding, Nathan pushed the bureau up against the door, realizing it would only buy him a matter of seconds.

"Sorry, dude, can't stay to talk!" Nathan exclaimed, picking up a chair and hurling it through the window. Shards of glass flew both in and out of the room. Nathan stepped up to the window and looked down.

"Damned Charlie's after you, ain't they?"

Nathan could not help himself and glanced back curiously at the man.

"What?"

The man patted his pillow, which lay on his chest. "Don't worry, bro, I got a surprise for them. Been keeping it from the nurses for a special occasion." The man stole a glance at the door, then back towards Nathan. "You best be goin'!"

Nathan shook his momentary lapse of reason and stepped up onto the air-conditioning unit in front of the now smashed window. He looked downwards and was about to change his mind as to the wisdom of this maneuver when...

The door crashed open, and Nathan heard the word "FREEZE!"

He took a half-glance backwards and saw the old cripple, with a smile on his face, clenching some sort of metal object between his teeth.

"*Sayonara!*" the man declared.

Nathan only had a split second to recognize the old-style grenade in the man's hand before he turned and leapt.

An ear-splitting explosion ripped through the room, and as he fell, he felt as if his whole body was on fire. He screamed momentarily, then felt an incredible jolt through his entire being.

Nathan gasped for breath, fully disoriented and realizing he was sopping wet. Rain beat down on him as he struggled to remember where he was. He could feel the damp grass and mud beneath him. His left arm was cold and numb. He felt stinging pain in his back from his shoulders to his buttocks. Nathan looked upwards to gaze upon the building which had been his home for several years. Three stories up, a fire was raging from one of the rooms. He looked towards the entrance of the building and read the words etched in stone, '*Veteran's Administration Hospital -- Damascus, Maryland*'.

Several men in suits burst through the front door with their handguns drawn. Suddenly, it all came back to him. He stood and immediately felt a sharp pain shoot up his back. He did his best to ignore it and hobbled towards the nearby woods.

Shots rang out, and Nathan felt the air rip past his ears. He reached the edge of a wooded area and hastened through the brush. Only then did he become aware that he was wearing nothing more than tattered rags.

As he scrambled through the woods, Nathan was able to discern the sound of dogs barking from quite a way behind him. He stopped only for a moment to catch his breath, then looked up to spot several moving lights up ahead. He realized that the wooded area ended no more than a half-kilometer farther. He glanced back momentarily as he heard the dogs gaining before resuming his flight.

Within a few minutes, he had reached the road. The dogs had become considerably louder, and it sounded as if an entire pack was following him. The rain beat down heavily on his face, and he ducked several times as the sound of intermittent gunfire continued.

He looked up and spotted a pair of headlights coming his way. Taking a brief look back in the direction of the barking, Nathan stepped out into the middle of the road, frantically waving his arms.

He heard the sound of a horn blaring and the screeching of multiple tires bracing themselves upon the asphalt. He quickly became aware that he had stepped out in front of an eighteen-wheeler, which now stood motionless no more than a meter in front of him. Nathan skipped around to the side and saw that the driver had already opened the door for him. He looked up at the trucker.

"¡Buenas noches, hermano!"

Nathan's eyes widened as he locked eyes with the Latino driver, who possessed a curious familiarity about him.

"I would suggest you step in, son," a voice from the back of the cab encouraged. "Eudagio speaks very little of your language, and I sense we do not have the luxury of excess time."

Nathan did as instructed, stepping up into the cab and pulling the door closed behind him.

"¡Vamos!" the voice from the back of the cab commanded as the driver smiled and nodded, engaging the gears of the vehicle.

"Thank you," Nathan managed, still out of breath. He looked to the back of the cab and saw a man with long hair and a beard that was even longer and knotted. Again, Nathan experienced a brief sense of familiarity, bordering on déjà vu, but he quickly shook it off.

"Really, thank you."

Eudagio again looked over to Nathan. "*¡Mi hermano! ¡Necesita ropas!*"

Nathan looked back to the shabby-looking man in the back for clarification. "It would seem that you are in need of clothing."

Nathan became aware of his virtual nakedness and looked down in embarrassment.

"No need to worry, son. We have some extra clothes in the back of the cab which might fit you."

Nathan looked up towards the man, still somewhat dazed. He had to stop himself from frowning as he was hit by a pungent odor. The man had obviously not showered in a few days.

"Thank you," he stated as he reached into the back of the cab.

"You're in for quite a ride, son."

Nathan pulled forward a pair of jeans and a sweatshirt.

"What?"

He waited for an answer, but the man briefly closed his eyes and began to whistle a song that Nathan did not recognize. After Nathan had pulled the jeans on, he extended an open hand towards the man in the back of the cab.

"My name's Nathan."

The man opened his eyes and smiled, reaching out his own hand. "It is good to meet you, Nathan. You have already met Eudagio here, and I am called Hanoch…"

ii

Alexandre Nesterov was doing his best to help his daughter keep it together. Since the incident three years ago, she had been unable to maintain a consistent train of thought. All the therapy and medicine in the world had been unable to stop her vivid and recurrent hallucinations. He had convinced her to stay the previous night at his place, to which she had reluctantly agreed.

The driver, Pavel Radchikov, turned the wheel gradually, making a left into the driveway that no longer led to a house. It was a glorious day; a good day to visit loved ones who had passed on.

As the limousine pulled closer to the path leading to the gravesites, they came across several police vehicles blocking the way.

"*Chto za huy!*" Nesterov muttered under his breath.

Radchikov was forced to stop the vehicle. An officer looked over towards them, then approached the driver's side, knocking on the glass. Radchikov obliged him by rolling down the window.

The officer looked at the driver briefly before turning his attention towards Vanya and Nesterov.

"I'm sorry, folks, but I'm going to have to ask you to turn around and leave this area."

Vanya watched the officer intently as a tear began to fall from her eye.

Nesterov responded in his usual tactful manner. "What the hell has happened here?"

The officer paused momentarily, obviously not pleased at Nesterov's tone or language. "I'm afraid there has been some vandalism here, nothing serious, but you're going to have to—"

Not interested in taking this conversation any further, Nesterov stepped out of the car and hastened towards the gravesite, seemingly oblivious to the officer's presence or authority.

"SIR! Stop what you're doing and…"

Nesterov did not wait to hear the officer out, and he was pretty comfortable with the fact that his men would keep him detained for the necessary time.

He stepped over the grassy knoll and spotted several more police officers rolling out a police line. There were a number of people talking and taking police photographs. Nesterov looked down at the parallel gravesites and gasped.

There, where his grandson Tobias Isaac had been buried, was a gaping hole.

The other gravesites were untouched, with the exception of the skeletal remains of an adult, almost completely intact, sprawled out across them. Shards of what was left of a small casket were scattered across a ten-meter radius.

TRYST

Nesterov slipped into a deep state of vertigo as phrases from those present bounced off his consciousness.

"...it's that Chardin boy's grave..."

"...no clue as to where these adult remains came from..."

"...you can see that a bullet hole entered through the back of the skull..."

Nesterov's eye was momentarily drawn to the out-of-place tree he had recalled from his other visits to this unhappy place. It had clearly grown a good deal more, but for the first time, he saw that it was completely bare.

"I understand..." he whispered, still encompassed by a surreal sense of existence, though not exactly sure why these words came to his lips.

A plain-clothes police officer approached, his badge hanging from his jacket pocket.

"Sir, what are you doing here? I'm going to have to ask you to—"

"I am the owner of this property! I demand to know what has happened here!"

The officer toned his voice down at this response and nodded in acknowledgement. He reached for his police-modified *iBerry*, touched the screen an few times, then held it out to Nesterov.

"If you would please sir, I would like to verify that claim."

Nesterov hesitated a moment, though his agitation superseded any significant sense of discretion. He placed his right thumb on the small screen. The *iBerry* beeped, then the officer held up the screen near to Nesterov's right eye. It beeped again.

The officer drew the device back, then looked at the screen. His eyes suddenly widened.

"I'm sorry, sir...ahhh... Mr. Nesterov. We received an anonymous tip this morning about some activity taking place here. We arrived about two hours ago and found this."

At that point another man dressed in white and obviously with forensics approached the two.

"I have some preliminary information, Detective," the man looked warily at Nesterov.

"It's okay. This man is the owner of the property," the officer instructed.

The man nodded in acknowledgement. "Well, first off, this grave was disturbed a long time ago. Someone has done some additional moving of dirt recently, but the dig here may be a year old, perhaps even more."

Nesterov looked confused.

"It has been a while since we have... have been here."

The man nodded. "Yes, well, that's just the beginning. These shards, the supposed broken pieces of a casket. The preliminary tests show they were actually broken apart even before that. I mean, we're talking at least fifteen years."

The detective frowned. "So the casket the boy was buried in broke apart years ago underground?"

With that, the forensic tech's confused expression peaked. "That's just it. We need to run more tests to get final results—the shards clearly have DNA on them, but there are no signs of decomposition. It just doesn't make sense."

The detective shook his head. "And the adult remains?"

"We should have definitive results back in a matter of—"

"TOBIAS!"

This last voice pierced Nesterov's unconscious reverie, and he spun around to see Vanya sprinting towards the gravesite, crying hysterically.

Nesterov moved quickly and grabbed his daughter before she nearly leapt right into the open grave. He pulled her close to him, trying to shield her from the grisly horror which lay in front of them.

"God no! Oh please, God... NO!"

iii

Paula walked down the hospital hallway, her heart thumping rapidly.

Paula, it would be good if you came home.

She had been home just two weeks before for her spring break—her *last* spring break—as she would be graduating from the University of Pennsylvania in a little more than a month. She had noted that her father has lost a lot of weight at the time, and he had developed a cough, that she now feared had become pneumonia. Her mother had informed her that he was going in for testing two days ago.

What's wrong, mom? Is it Dad?

Just come home, honey.

She had driven through the night—not a big problem with the vehicle automation these days—but she had almost wished she *did* have to concentrate on the road—on anything—to keep her mind from dwelling on the continually emerging morbid thoughts.

Paula reached room 316 on the right, taking a deep breath before stepping in.

Her father lay on the bed, her mother holding his hand and talking softly. He turned towards Paula, a gentle smile emerging, while her mother's eyes filled with tears.

"Hello, Punkin…"

His voice was weak. He had lost more weight, to the point where it was clear that this was not good. Paula walked over to the chair on the opposite side of the bed from her mother and sat down. She took a quick look around the room.

"Where is—"

"He's with my mother, Paula. I thought—"

But Paula would not let her mother finish as she turned to her father. She was unable to contain the note of anxiety in her voice.

"What is it, Dad? What's going on?"

Her mother looked to him, "Marcus, maybe we sh—"

"It's okay, Avila," he responded, looking with compassion at his spouse. "Paula's not a little girl anymore." Paula's eyes widened as her father looked back to her and continued. "It's the virus, Punkin, the H-virus. Apparently it's been in me for some time." He chuckled softly, which struck Paula as odd considering the news he just shared, and momentarily closed his eyes as a coughing fit ensued. Paula grabbed a hold of his free hand.

"It's okay, Punkin." He cleared his throat, then continued. "Anyway, I thought I was dieting… thought I could stand to lose a few pounds. I guess the weight loss wasn't due to my great self-discipline."

Paula was struggling for words. "I-I don't understand how you could get it. I don't…" Suddenly, a thought struck her. "It was that man, wasn't it? The one you picked up who was lying on the side of the road in Honduras." Paula looked at her mother in dismay as the scene replayed itself in her head. "He was emaciated and had all those sores covering him. You… you must have had a cut or something."

Her father looked at her in a conciliatory fashion. "We can't be sure of that, Paula. There could be a number of possibilities for this. And even so, I would not trade that mission trip for anything. It gave me back my faith. For more than twenty years since Therese died, I was walking around like a man without hope. Now I am overflowing with it."

Paula looked at her mother dumbstruck, then back to her father. "Hope? What do you mean 'hope'? You just told me you have the H-virus. It's not curable, it's—"

"All things are possible with God, honey," her mother said, though not with great conviction.

Paula was clearly incensed. "God? Are you kidding, Mom? Dad was doing God's work in Honduras, and this is what God gives him?"

Her father gently interjected. "We can't understand the ways of God."

"Damn right we can't!" Her eyes were filling up now. Both parents were caught off-guard by her outburst. Though they knew she had been struggling to some degree with her faith since she left for college, this language was still uncharacteristic. Paula did not hesitate, but continued with her imputation. "He took away a sister I never got to know! And where was He that day at *The Phoenix* concert?"

They each sat there in a moment of silence, both mother and father knowing that theological explanations would not help at this juncture. Paula had her arms folded, looking down as the tears started to roll down her cheeks. Suddenly, there was a spark in her eye.

"Wait. What about that man they call 'The Prophet' out in India? I've been following him in my internship. I've listened to him speak… and I've seen some of the unexplainable occurrences that he has manifested. There have been healings reported as well. Dad, we could—"

But her father gently shook his head. "No, Paula. I'm not going down that road. I am at peace with this, I am—"

"What?" Paula was incensed. "Those apparition sites are good enough for you, but not this real-live healer?"

Following their mission trip to Honduras, her parents had visited Lourdes, Fátima, and several other sites on a pilgrimage across Europe where the Blessed Mother has purportedly appeared. They had called it a 'vacation of thanksgiving'… for her father's recovery of his faith.

"Punkin, that trip was just in gratitude to Our Lady for drawing me back to the faith. You and your mom stuck with it all these years, but I was spiritually dead. I had to thank her, and I did not ask anything more of her… nor do I now, unless it is within her Son's will."

There was again a period of silence. Then Paula spoke up, her voice quivering with both sadness and anger. "So what are they telling you? How long are they saying?"

Avila was about to speak, but Marcus squeezed her hand. "It seems I have one of the most aggressive strains, Punkin. It's all in God's hands now."

Paula put her hand up to her face, trying to restrain an impulse to cry out. Her mother spoke.

"Father Tyler is on his way right now—"

"Uncle Tyler?" Paula snapped. "What's he coming here for? He's the one that put the stupid idea in your head for us to go to Honduras!"

With that, Paula broke down completely, wailing over the imminent loss of her father, perhaps sensing that it would take from her so much more.

6

And it came to pass that some of the life forms tended more towards the essence of the Physical Entity, while others favored that of the Spiritual. Those who pursued the physical essence were called *Čidentůl,* [1] and those favoring the spiritual essence were known as *Řeintůl.* [2] And this was thought to be good, for it provided diversity and identity among the life forms, from which could emerge a synergistic effect that neither entity could have provided outside of the other.

Leviat D: 1-3
Book of Given Truths

---

[1] Literally, "Westerner"
[2] Literally, "Easterner"

i

Siro Scribner trudged vigilantly behind his guide, who freely swung his machete, slashing through the thick foliage. The relentless African sun beat down heavily upon the pair, and Siro was parched, having foolishly consumed his entire water supply hours earlier.

It had been a trying several days. The first day was easy enough, landing a commercial jet in "free" Malta (the Sicilian Mafia and their families had fled here in the midst of the Islamic Revolution, and the Caliph felt that he had much more pressing matters to attend to in the immediate future.) The same day, he was smuggled into Africa via a single prop plane to a destination somewhere seven hundred kilometers to the south. Even the subsequent daylong ride in the jeep was not all that bad. But the past two days of hiking through a world completely devoid of rest stops had been the pits. Siro's insides gurgled and shifted as he struggled to avoid another bout with his screaming intestines through sheer willpower.

As they stepped over exotic insects and ducked under poisonous vines, Siro tried to recapture the excitement he had felt upon learning of the possible location of Jimi T. Expo. Still, a twinge of guilt grasped him tightly. It was the first information he had ever paid for—bribing a clerk at the AmeriCorps office in D.C. Even more so, he was fully aware of the fact that he was violating an international quarantine by entering the Sub-Saharan African continent. He hoped he would be able to find a way to rationalize it all to himself in the end.

The first six locations they had visited were a bust—at least as far as locating his prey. Still, each had had contact with the man they referred to as the "Shadow King", and without exception, these villages had made recent and unprecedented jumps into prosperity. But what was even more astonishing was that in each case the villagers insisted that they had been cured of the dreaded H-virus disease by this man. Their outward appearance of health seemed to confirm their claims to be true.

"Up ahead, boss!" the guide called out.

"What was that, Emmanuel?" Siro called back, wiping the thick, dirt-infested sweat from his brow.

"Ahead, boss, clearing, Zoso village."

Siro looked up and could clearly see a break in the dense jungle. He produced a smile of relief as they moved forward another fifty meters, finding themselves at the edge of a clearing.

He watched as several natives approached them, smiling peacefully. Emmanuel spoke several words to them, and Siro witnessed initial expressions of affirmation slowly transform into slight looks of sadness, as the natives shot glances towards him. A moment later the natives, more and more displaying visible signs of distress, gestured northward. Siro noticed the odd discoloration on the back of each of the villager's right hands, like a peculiar-looking "C".

There was some final discussion and multiple nervous glances continued to be directed towards Siro. Finally, Emmanuel made an obvious gesture of thanks, and he proceeded to move in a northerly direction. Siro met eyes briefly with the three natives before following his guide.

When the greeting natives were out of earshot, Siro leaned up towards

Emmanuel's ear. "What was that all about? What did they say?"

Emmanuel looked back at Siro somewhat curiously. "They say, boss, follow children, they take us to Shadow King."

"But why did they look so bummed out?"

Emmanuel gazed back at Siro, suddenly appearing somewhat troubled himself.

"They fear that you here to take their king away." He hesitated for a moment, uncomfortably, then spoke again. "That why you here, boss? Take Shadow King from the people?"

Siro was dumbfounded. "I-I well... no," and he suddenly had to stop—now wondering to himself, *What is my intention?*

He had not thought about it. He had been so bent and determined to track down this enigma, to crack the story of a lifetime, that he had never given much thought as to what he would do if he actually *found* the man.

The pair continued without another word up the side of a hill, as several Zoso children shot past them, giggling. Siro and Emmanuel reached the crest of the hill, looked across the landscape below, and froze in their footsteps.

Before them, a hundred or so Zoso children sat, circled around a single Caucasian man. The children up close clung to the man as he passed out small pieces of food and sang to them in their native tongue. The mass of children appeared spellbound, hanging on every melodic note that came forth from this man's lips. At different points in the song, the children would spontaneously call out in unison before again falling silent, listening absorbedly to their Shadow King.

The man wore garments like the natives, and his skin had become a smooth olive-brown thanks to the intense African sun. His hair was jet black, and he wore a ring on his left hand with a large red stone that shone brilliantly, almost as if it had its own source of illumination. But the oddest part of this picture was something else. The man wore a dark pair of old-style (though not inexpensive) sunglasses which accentuated the surreality of the scene.

As Siro gawked at the sight, he slowly became aware of the children shuffling to each side, collectively creating a path straight through from him to their 'King'. They called out in unison again.

"Go, boss," Emmanuel whispered in Siro's ear.

On the verge of being overcome with trepidation, yet still fully exhilarated by the situation, Siro took a step forward. He made his way through the human aisle created for him as the children called out and the Shadow King continued to sing. Their collective voices reached a crescendo as Siro stepped to within two meters of the man, and then cut off abruptly.

Siro stood there, motionless, feeling as if he were going to drown in the utter silence. He sensed all eyes focusing upon him as he finally garnered enough strength to speak.

"M-Mr. Expo, Mr. Jimi T. Expo?"

The man looked intently at Siro, who sensed his penetrating gaze from even behind the sunglasses. As the children watched with baited breath, their Shadow King slowly stood from the rock on which he had been seated. The two stood face to face momentarily, and finally the slightest hint of a smile emerged on the visage of the great enigma of the modern day.

"And so it begins."

ii

"Is it a sin, Father? To pull away from this dark world?"

Annie D. sat across the table, sipping the tea which Father Daniel Ananias had made for her. She had attended Mass earlier that afternoon, over which he had presided. The celebration of *The Annunciation,* where the Angel Gabriel had first spoken to the Virgin Mary and asked if she would be willing to bear the Son of God in her womb had always held a special place in her heart.

Aye, the humility of God.

Father Daniel had noted Annie D's uncharacteristically despondent disposition this day and had invited her over after the conclusion of the Mass. The question she posed to him was far from unique in these times. He gazed across the table, curiously.

"If you speak of giving up hope, then yes, it could be an act against charity. But you must understand, Annie, that either way, the void your withdrawal creates will not remain a void; it will more likely than not be filled with a much darker spirit, especially in the present day."

Annie D. offered a sad chuckle. "Aye, not unlike our country, yes, Father? We withdraw from the world, and every form of evil, just waitin' for us to leave, closes in." She leaned forward as if to share a secret. "Not sayin' we were a bastion of goodness ourselves!"

Father Daniel nodded solemnly. These had been tough years. Despite the recent dramatic increase in prosperity in the United States, the rest of the world seemed to be unraveling. Even at home, attendance at Mass had been on the decline for decades. His friend, President Hugh Jennings Lang, had been able to initiate much change that was good, though he seemed to be powerless to stem the tide against any form of faith—especially Christianity. Father Daniel's sense from prayer was that things were to get worse... a *lot* worse.

"More tea?"

Annie D. nodded, and Father Daniel lifted the kettle with his left hand (the arthritis in his right had become near unbearable), pouring the remaining tea into Annie's cup.

"Have you spoken to your daughter recently?"

"Aye, I speak to Vanya nearly every day—she's a rare being, Father. I feel like there is a wedge between us. I'd like to live closer, but the stubborn girl's insistent that I not be." Despite her downcast sentiments, Annie D. chuckled as she cocked her eyebrow towards Father Daniel. "There's an old sayin', 'a son's a son till he finds a wife, a daughter's a daughter for the rest of her life.' I suppose Vanya breaks that tradition."

Father Daniel hesitated. "And your husband?"

Annie's face grew more solemn. "As for the man I married, it's a case of the final straw that broke the camel's back. Somethin' broke inside of me when it all happened. I feel I just saw him—perhaps just permitted myself to see him—for who he really is. I had to pull away. No, Father, I'll not divorce the man, but I can't be layin' eyes on him again, I just can't. It seems the world has moved on, and so have I."

Yes, it has moved on to a darker frame. Father Daniel was puzzled by the phrase which entered his consciousness. His visions and clarity in contemplation had ended abruptly three years ago. There was no longer consolation when he prayed, only an interior struggle. It was as if a switch had been flipped off. Yet still, he knew of what Annie D. spoke; he sensed legions were gathering on either side. What was most disconcerting to him, however, was that the battle lines were becoming more and more blurred, so much so that it was becoming difficult to tell where anyone stood.

Lord, do not abandon me now. I sense the dark night; strengthen me for the sake of Your flock!

iii

Nathan stepped from the cab of the eighteen-wheeler. It had been an interesting two days to say the least. They had driven until midnight that first evening, when both Eudagio and the man called Hanoch made it clear that they would rest, claiming the day to be a holy one. The same behavior was apparently true for the next day, a Sunday, and then they resumed their trek shortly after midnight.

Nathan thought the whole business curious, but took the opportunity to rest nonetheless—despite the invitations to attend church with the pair— allowing the last vestiges of whatever drugs were in his system to dissipate. There had not been a great deal of conversation—at least not conversation that Nathan could understand—though he had gathered that Hanoch was some type of religious holy man, and that Eudagio was some recent convert, apparently having a life-changing experience after some sort of terrible accident of which he was the cause.

Though Nathan had not had a particular destination in mind when he hitched the ride with the pair, he was pleasantly surprised to find that their travels were to pass within thirty kilometers of Nathan's hometown, Pergamum. Eudagio was kind enough to take Nathan to the only place he could conceive of finding a friend.

Nathan bid goodbye and thanks to Hanoch, who provided a steady look of concern. Eudagio provided a big smile. "*¡Vaya con Dios!*"

As the rescuing pair pulled away, Nathan stood staring while the truck slowly vanished into the pre-dawn mist. He rubbed his eyes, and then turned, finding himself at the edge of the gravel driveway leading to the house of Simon Wilson.

He felt it was better to be dropped off here as opposed to Jonathan's house, as he was still leery as to the situation with Jonathan and Nesterov.

It took a moment to get his feet to move; a strange tickle began to dance within his innards.

Get a grip, big guy. They don't get any more harmless than Simon.

And just as quickly as it emerged, the sensation was gone. Nathan walked up to the house, slowly, methodically. He took a deep breath and knocked on the door.

At first there was no sound at all. It was still a few hours before daybreak, yet he somehow felt a sense of urgency. He was about to knock again when he saw a light come on inside. Soft footsteps approached the door.

"Who is it?" the voice asked hoarsely.

"It's Nathan. Simon, open the door, it's freezing out here!"

There was a long pause, and Nathan's anxiety gave way to annoyance.

"Open the damn door, Simon!"

"Go away."

The utterance was barely audible, but no one could mistake the resonance of fright in Simon's voice. Still, Nathan had slipped past the point of empathy.

"Son of a b—"

Nathan cursed as he butted his shoulder into the door once... twice... three times before it busted in. As he burst through the doorway, he grabbed onto the figure in front of him. Both he and Simon sprawled to the floor.

"God no! Please no! Please—"

Nathan sat up, straddling Simon, who was now on his back. He pulled Simon up by the collar of his T-shirt. "What the hell has gotten into you?"

Simon gasped for breath, finally making eye contact with Nathan. His struggling ceased and a look of astonishment emerged from his face.

"Nathan!" he gasped. "Oh God, Nathan! I thought you were dead!"

Nathan stared back at his friend in disbelief.

Simon's panting slowed as he choked out, "They said you were dead..."

iv

"Speak your deepest desires, my children, for the *Kôles* rewards he that is faithful to his master!"

The millions surrounded Tæsír Hoc, emaciated from thirst and malnutrition. Though not a man spoke, he knew their need. Thousands of parched kilometers of land surrounded them for as far as the eye could see. Not a single drop of water had fallen from the sky in over a generation throughout the vast majority of the land of India. The drought had now spread to Pakistan, Afghanistan, and even parts of China. In a mere twenty years, the population of this one nation had been reduced by nearly a fifth.

The Prophet closed his eyes, and then spoke.

"All that has life answers to the *Kôles*. We, as children of the *Kôles*, possess the means to command that which is subject to Her. We *all* have the sixth sense, we *all* have second sight, we *all* have the power to move mountains by sheer will!"

As if on cue, the sound of thunder struck, reverberating throughout the land. The millions who had a moment before stared listlessly at this so-called prophet suddenly found a spark of hope in their souls.

"Ask for it, my children!" the Prophet commanded. "Believe in the gift of the *Kôles*, and it is yours. Do you believe, my children?"

A resounding "YES!" in their native tongue shook the Earth with even greater conviction than the thunder. The sky flashed red, then purple, then white. The ground continued to rumble as the Tæsír whispered through clenched teeth, "Let there be *LIFE!*"

And suddenly, from two hundred kilometers away, a jet stream of ocean water propelled up through the air. The millions looked to the heavens as the stream of seawater shot through the sky with the speed of lightning then exploded above them. They were instantly baptized in a deluge of water.

A moment later, amidst coughing, splashing, and laughter, the Prophet raised his hands into the air. The fresh water (clearly desalinated on its journey to this place) instantly sunk into the soil, miraculously creating a land now rich and fertile.

"For it is written," the Prophet intimated, "'I will lead them to springs of life-giving water, and I will wipe every tear from their eyes.' Go now, my brothers and sisters, receive the Seal, then return to plant new life. Your faith has healed you."

7

Philadelphia Enquirer   ~

ZAIRE - Sub-Saharan Africa enters its ninth year of quarantine today with no indications given that the global restrictions will be lifted in the foreseeable future. The current H-virus positive population there has risen to 57%. Nearly 270 million deaths have been attributed to the disease on this continent alone.

Last month, following great pressure from the embattled Islamic Union, Libya became the final African-Arab nation to be removed from the U.N. quarantine. According to the report supplied by the U.N.'s World Health and Security Council, it was determined that Libya had undertaken "appropriate and sufficient" border control measures, as well as implemented an "acceptable containment policy" for those within the country.

While unsubstantiated reports from within quarantined Sub-Saharan Africa have suggested that entire tribes have been cured of the virus, the same Council is viewing these reports as nothing more than an attempt to have the quarantine lifted prematurely. Still, members of the Council have secretly acknowledged that their ability to enforce any of these resolutions continues to decline.

Despite strictly enforced precautions, the worldwide H-virus rate has risen to 29%.

i

Nathan stared at Simon in disbelief, his coffee cup nearly slipping from his trembling hands.

"No, no, it can't be… it can't…"

Simon shook his head and wiped his eyes. "No, man, it's true. He was electrocuted. The feds say it was sabotage. I don't know. I tried to stop the fire… I tried. It was just too much."

Nathan shook his head still denying the words, yet somehow sensing with certainty that Simon spoke the truth. Simon again moved to wipe his intermittent tears, removing his wire-rim glasses with his left hand and wiping with this right. Nathan's eyes were caught by the somewhat unnatural movement. He focused his eyes and realized that where Simon's right hand should be was an artificial limb.

Simon caught Nathan's eye and shamefully realized what he was looking at. He lowered his hand below the table and breathed a heavy sigh. "I guess I should have known better than to try to put a fire out with my hand. I-I guess I wasn't thinking all that good at the time."

Simon cursed under his breath in an unfamiliar fashion.

Nathan's eyes widened as he bit his lower lip. "Oh Simon, I…" Nathan stopped himself momentarily, at a loss for words. "What did I…" he began, still stumbling. "I don't… Jon was…"

"He's dead," Simon stated solemnly. "Damned bastards killed him." At this point Simon's face crinkled up as he fought the images seared in his mind. "It was so hot… it was so quick… there was almost nothing left…"

He hesitated for a moment, pulling himself together. Then looking towards the door he said, "At the hospital, I heard some feds talking, said these dudes that did it were really after *you*… and… and that… that they were successful."

Nathan again felt a wave of confusion.

That's not right!

No, none of it was right, and he knew it. Something was wrong that night—*very* wrong—and Jonathan had sensed it. From the moment they met that talent agent, Jonathan had somehow sensed that all was not as it should be.

Nathan mulled over the situation, concluding that Simon was attempting to be truthful with him, even though it was also clear that there was much Simon did *not* know. Though his own mind was still not fully lucid, Nathan realized that his friend had been fed a great deal of misinformation.

"I shouldn't have come here," Nathan stated.

Simon looked confused. "What do you mean?"

"I've put you in danger," he professed, finally looking up and making eye contact with Simon. "They're going to be coming for me."

Simon looked perplexed. "What are you talking about?"

As Nathan was about to speak, they heard the sound of tires moving across Simon's gravel driveway.

Nathan held up his hand to prevent Simon from speaking any further. The sound stopped. He thought for a moment. The driveway began about a quarter of a kilometer from the house and came around a bend only ten meters from the front door.

Nathan got up and peeked out the window. He could not see any cars yet. He looked back to Simon.

"Is there another way out?" he asked impatiently.

Simon still looked unconvinced, apparently not being able to fully digest the gravity of their situation. He shrugged his shoulders. "My Uncle Garf's house is about a kilometer through the woods. But, dude, really I don't see wh—"

"Let's go," Nathan interrupted, pulling Simon less-than-gently by the arm. Simon resisted momentarily, and Nathan swung around, bringing the two face to face. "I have no time to explain. They've already tried to kill me once. We have to get out of here. NOW!"

Simon hesitated for a moment, wide-eyed and trying to ascertain the current sanity of his old friend, then he slowly nodded his head. As Nathan released him and stepped towards the back door, Simon took one last brief look around his house. A strange feeling arose in him, a certain awareness that he would never see this place again.

He started to move, but then a thought struck him. Simon moved across the kitchen to a ceramic jar situated high above his cupboards, and after pulling a small bag from it, he placed the jar back in its previous resting place.

TRYST

"Come on, Simon!" Nathan whispered through gritted teeth.

Simon turned, glanced briefly at his artificial hand, then slipped out the back door with Nathan.

ii

President Hugh Jennings Lang couldn't sleep. Three clandestine assassination attempts in less than a month had him, understandably, on edge. The Secret Service, along with what could be described in no manner other than Divine intervention, had not only kept him alive, but stopped the would-be perpetrators in their tracks before any news of the attempts were even able to be made public. What had most concerned him, though, were the backgrounds—and subsequently perceived motives—of these men. Three Chinese nationals sporting Buddhist tattoos. Seven others from various nations within the Islamic Union. And then one loner who had ties back to the now defunct Irish Republican Militia—of course, wearing a brown scapular. It was so... so *predictable*.

Things did not sit right with him. What would the implications be if any of these attempts were successful? Attempts to discredit him in a scandal had been fruitless. Yet surely, those who opposed him recognized they could neither afford to make a martyr of him nor of his cause. Still, if any of these particular plots were successful, Lang's moves against America's isolationism and attempts to curb the growing religious intolerance could easily be framed as naïve, even dangerous.

But it still doesn't add up, it doesn't fit their agenda.

Lang's recent discovery, and subsequent dismantling, of a covert governmental program which mass-produced a genetically engineered grain with a contraceptive element to it had seemed to be the final straw. The grain was being shipped to specifically targeted impoverished areas, as well as the majority of the Third World. Of course, there was no indication of who had authorized this program, or how long in had been running.

In any case, Lang knew he needed some time to get his head together, as he found himself starting to make decisions out of fear—starting to second guess all of his actions.

So he had brought his wife and two grown daughters with him to

Camp David for the weekend. His vice president, J. Walker Shrubb, a long-time friend and confidant, was more than willing to provide coverage for Lang to take the time. Lang's oldest daughter carried his first grandchild in her womb. They had just learned she was to have a boy.

The president slipped out of his bed, leaving his wife to what appeared to be her first restful night in weeks, and then stepped into the bathroom, quietly closing the door.

Father Daniel bolted up in bed, calling out with a guttural cry, "Good Lord! No!"

The explosion sent Hugh Lang, still clutching the bathroom doorknob, airborne. He felt the hot air simultaneously brush against him with the force of the impact as his skin was instantly singed. Lang landed a moment later on soft ground, knocking the wind out of him, as the remains of the door crumbled about him. As he gasped for breath, he looked up to see what was left of the cottage that held his wife and daughters engulfed in flames.

"No," he whispered in desperation, still fighting for breath. "Please God, no…"

iii

"NOW!"

The lead man kicked in the door, and a half-dozen others shot in through the entrance, guns drawn. Jake Hanssen slipped in cautiously behind them. He looked toward the staircase, nodded his head, and three men bolted upstairs.

Several men who had come through the back door entered the foyer. The first looked at Hanssen and shook his head.

"The basement," Hanssen whispered through gritted teeth.

A minute later, the men who had searched the upstairs came down, also shaking their heads.

"Nothing, sir."

TRYST

Hanssen clenched his jaw and ran his fingers through his ever-thinning hair. The men returned from the basement with the same response.

Hanssen pulled out his two-way radio, barking into it. "Anything out there, Lydon?"

Digital static cracked across the radio for a moment. "Not much, Hanssen, but it does look like someone came through these woods out back within the past few hours."

Hanssen thought for a moment. "Coming or going?"

The voice cracked back. "Definitely going, and at a pretty good pace."

At that moment, several more of Hanssen's men entered the room. "Somebody's been here within the past half-hour. There's a small bottle of tonic water out, cooler than room temperature, and warm coffee."

Hanssen nodded, a spark of positive feelings re-entering his world. "Get some prints." He hesitated for just a moment, and then got back on the two-way radio. "All right, Lydon, we're moving out from here. Leave a few men to watch the house, and we'll follow that trail. He's close, and he's got Wilson with him."

8

I'm so tired
Of this fight
I can't tell
Wrong from right

Just what God
Is this for?
Is this our own
Holy War?

– Jimi T. Expo
Holy War

i

Nathan looked over at Simon, who kept his eyes glued to the road. Simon initially had not been real up on the idea of "borrowing" his uncle's wheels, but he had quickly realized that they did not have much of a choice. The old Saturn they swiped was practically a classic, and the ignition, along with a number of other features, had been modified in some form or another.

"You sure your uncle won't call the police?"

"Dude, of that, you can be confident. He's one of those anti-government types. I may be a libertarian, but he goes way beyond that. Even this car has a number of 'special features', or, umm… maybe better put, has *removed* a number of special features."

"What do you mean?"

Simon looked over at Nathan with an expression that could only be described as one of misgiving. "Dude, what do you mean, 'what do you mean?' Where the hell you been?"

Nathan frowned, glancing out the window. "Out, I guess."

Simon looked over at Nathan, realizing that his friend was not attempting to pull his leg. "You're serious, aren't you? You really have been out, haven't you?"

Nathan looked back at him, somewhat irritated. "Well?"

Simon looked at him steadily before continuing. "I'm sorry, Nathan. Not long after the… the accident, Congress passed a law that any future automobiles produced must have the *i-Nav* navigation system installed. It's kind of like GPS on steroids, using satellites, cellular towers, and a series of sensors within the car and road to get you from one place to another without doing a thing."

"You mean a car that drives itself?"

"Exactly, but it's even more than that. All roads in the United States have been fully mapped, including elevation and type of surface, by a company called InnerMap. All cars, even those purchased earlier and that are not fully automated, are still required to have this navigation system in them. Because the tracking and sensing is three-deep, again, the satellite, the towers, and the onboard sensors, it is virtually foolproof. All roads are now covered with sensors as well. The system knows every car, everyone's speed, every destination, every area of road construction… so the result? And, dude, this is the coolest, you plug in your destination, then let the car do the rest—and no accidents. They say accidents have decreased 97% in the past two years, and all those that have happened have been in cars without the full system."

Nathan nodded curiously. "Kind of takes the fun out of driving. So what does that have to do with this car?"

"Well, like I said," Simon continued. "My Uncle Garf is not a fan of the government, and he quickly saw this whole system as a way not to just manage traffic and avoid accidents, but as one more way for Big Brother to track people and their movements. So he, being the modern mechanic he is—which essentially means he's a computer programmer—rigged this particular car so it couldn't be tracked."

Nathan took a moment to reflect on this good fortune, considering their situation. "That's perfect, Simon. I'll have to send a thank you card to your uncle."

As he continued to ponder this intriguing invention, Nathan reached over and flipped the satellite radio on. Simon continued to focus on the road, not responding. Nathan began to flip through the stations, then suddenly stopped.

A familiar song came out across the speakers, though he was not quite sure where he had heard it before:

Help me now 'cause I think I'm falling…
…my mind keeps screaming NO!
Help me now, it's the Four Winds calling…
…How can I dream when the flesh is gone?

"What is this?" he inquired, as if in a pleasant reverie.

Simon shook his head, looking at Nathan with a slight smile of confusion. "Man, this is going to take some time getting used to. It's like you're Rip Van Winkle." He focused his eyes back on the road, a slightly sad expression coming across his face. He spoke again, beginning with a curse. "It's Jimi T. Expo. Dude's the biggest thing since Elvis Presley."

Nathan was perplexed, still not accustomed to Simon's newly acquired vocabulary. "Wait a minute, I know that name…"

Simon nodded. "You should. Three years ago it seemed like he was the only thing that stood between us and the big time."

Nathan looked over to Simon, on the verge of full realization.

Simon nodded again, producing an expression nearing revulsion. "After the accident, LaVey had no choice but to sign him."

"Damn," Nathan responded, almost in shock. "We lose everything, and this man takes the world by storm!"

Simon shook his head absently. "He's a strange bird though, that's for sure. Nobody, 'cept LaVey, had seen hide nor hair of him—'till *today*. Mr. Jimi T. is supposed to be having a press conference this morning. It's been leaked that he's going to announce that he's forming a band and that he's joining some cult following."

Nathan shook his head, attempting to pull himself out of the daze he had fallen into. As much as he hated to admit it, he kind of liked the music.

The song completed, and Simon reached down, shutting the radio off. He looked over towards Nathan. "I'm… I'm not much into music anymore. Kind of lost its appeal."

Nathan noticed Simon's hands, well, *hand* trembling and decided to let it go. A few minutes later, Simon looked over at him again.

"So are you going to tell me what that was all about back at my house, and exactly who's after you?"

"Us," Nathan mumbled.

"What?"

"Us, they're after us now."

"Great, this is just great. You want to tell me who?"

Nathan shook his head. "In good time, Simon. In good time."

There was a long silence, which Simon again broke.

"So where to now?"

Nathan thought for a moment, then returned Simon's stare. "I think I need to see Mrs. Storm...ahh... Jon's aunt."

"You mean mother."

Nathan was about to correct Simon but decided against it. "Yeah, whatever. I just need to figure out how I can safely get to her. Is she still living at the house?"

Simon shook his head. "No, she left almost immediately after the accident. Moved out to the Midwest—Missouri actually. She gave me her address... wouldn't let me write it down though. Made me memorize it. Said she thought I might need it."

Nathan nodded, obviously pleased. "Then I guess we're off."

"... to see the wizard..."

Nathan looked at Simon and smiled as he shook his head. "You should've worked on that sense of humor over these last three years."

ii

Siro sat at the table next to the podium. In front of him sat perhaps three-dozen reporters, each hand-selected by Jimi T. Expo. Despite the small audience, this press conference would be televised across the world.

A feeding frenzy had taken place at twelve o'clock this morning when Jimi T. Expo's third music disc, *Something Borrowed,* was released. An estimated seventy-two million copies had already been sold up to this point. Even the attempt on the president's life, which had sadly claimed the lives of his wife and two daughters, was not sufficient to divert the attention of the world from this momentous event.

Siro had had the benefit of listening to the music disc prior to its release. In fact, he had been granted many privileges since his discovery of Jimi T. Expo's whereabouts. Instead of being angry with him, which Siro would have understood (after all, he destroyed the man's self-imposed exile), Jimi T. was intensely positive about the situation, as well as their future collaboration.

Jimi T. had introduced Siro to the Prophet of the Modern Age, Tæsír Hoc, and at that moment, whatever had seemed important in Siro's life the day before felt like nothing more than the old cravings of a spoiled child. He had found *purpose* in life.

As Siro sat admiring his newly acquired "birthmark" on the back of his right hand, Jimi T. Expo entered the room from the left. A hush fell across the chamber.

The so-called "Mystic King" reached the podium, and Siro sensed him surveying the room intently from behind those dark glasses.

"Good day, my brothers and sisters, my name is Jimi T. Expo."

He spoke with a subtle, yet still clearly discernable, English accent, which seemed to catch many of the listeners off-guard.

"I would first like to offer my condolences to the president and those close to his family. Though I am greatly saddened by this tragedy, it serves as a fitting backdrop—an accurate display of the current situation in the world—of which I mean to speak with you today."

He breathed visibly, appearing to glance down momentarily as if truly moved by this event, then looked back up to the crowd. "I stand before you today, on the brink of the Modern Age, to announce an alliance of truth. As has been evident to most of you, the music I have produced in the past has often spoken of geopolitics and other worldly matters. With the exception of one particular piece, you will find that *Something Borrowed* continues along that same line of thinking, for as even recent events have highlighted, the politics of our world are of great consequence."

The audience sat mesmerized, savoring the passion which underlay each word from this man's lips.

"However," Jimi T. continued. "With the release of the single *Holy War*, which you will find to be quite different from the other pieces, I am bringing to a close this stage of my composing career and am now charting a new direction for my followers."

He paused, appearing for a brief moment as if he actually grew in stature. "While it may be difficult for many to accept, we must acknowledge what we have, in the very depths of our souls, known for many years." He again paused, not in apprehension, but as one who had the unenviable task of telling a friend that a loved one had died. "I share this without presumption, but with a note of clarity and urgency. The time has come to bring to a close the religions of our world, which have lost their significance, only to become a hindrance to the evolution of humanity upon the Earth. We see even today what Religionists have the capacity to do. Today, I announce my alliance with the one true knowledge, not a religion but a reality, which has arbitrarily been dubbed: *The Way of Mystic Realism*. Its title is of little importance, but its meaning and purpose are the most essential concepts in the history of existence."

What may indeed have been considered pretentious and even arrogant in years past was clearly being received with a spirit most akin to... *relief*. Siro smiled, feeling the power of the Life-Force dance within him as his great savior continued to speak.

"Over the next calendar year, I will begin assembling the greatest musicians of our time to produce the music and the very soul of The Way. I will not speak to you again until the time when all have been selected. Until then, I leave you to begin your own discovery of the truth. Standing to my left is Brother Siro, senior editor-in-chief of *The Signs of the Times*, which is the official publication of The Way of Mystic Realism."

A round of applause spontaneously erupted from the chamber. Siro smiled confidently and nodded to the audience. When the warm reception had died down, Jimi T. spoke again.

"And entering from my right, I am honored to present to you the Prophet of the Modern Age, the Great Teacher of Mystic Realism, Tæsír Hoc. Brothers and sisters, I bid you farewell."

Siro glanced to his right as the Prophet approached the podium. Though carrying a distinguished regality beyond all else present, save Jimi T., the Tæsír wore nothing more than a simple off-white cassock. The Prophet and Jimi T. clasped both hands, nodding reverently to each other. As Jimi T. stood to the side, the Prophet stepped up to the podium. He looked out across the chamber and smiled.

"It is a good day to be with you, brothers and sisters. Today is the Day of Enlightenment for the Western world, for today is the day that the newly translated texts, known as the *Book of Given Truths*, are released for all who wish to cultivate their personal and communal growth. These texts have been translated from ancient Mayan manuscripts and preserved by seekers of truth for many ages. Quite simply, they reveal the purpose of our existence and the implications thereof."

The Prophet's smile grew wider, as did the intensity with which he spoke. "We are on the brink of a great transformation, my brothers and sisters. The Way of Mystic Realism is simply a new paradigm—the *final* paradigm—which transcends religion and philosophy, being based not in myth, but in both social and spiritual truths. The Promised One, whom the texts contend will lead us into the Modern Age, is here among us."

At this moment, Tæsír Hoc turned to Jimi T. Expo and extended his arms. "Make straight the path of the One."

iii

The final sliver of the setting sun descended on the western horizon of the Isle of Patmos. A few of the several hundred souls preparing for the initiation of the sacred Triduum still remained outside the Chapel of St. John.

"It is not appropriate that I go in," Ibn insisted. "Though I admire the teachings of the good prophet Jesus, I am not a Christian. What happens here does not concern or involve me. My attendance would be incendiary."

Though his body was covered with sores and crippled to the point of paralysis, one could not mistake the frown on Ecumenical Patriarch Andreas II's face. Pope Peter II offered a sympathetic smile.

"It is understandable, Ibn, your apprehension. But I see that my brother is in agreement with me. Yes, we share different, and at times opposing, understandings of our Creator. Yet in truth, I see that God shows no partiality. In every nation, whoever fears Him and acts uprightly, is favorable to Him." Peter paused only for a moment, then continued. "Creating additional barriers would not serve charity. What is about to take place, what I *pray* will take place here in these few days as we begin the Sacred Triduum, will have implications for eternity. I do not wish to enter this new era being a poor host!"

"Why would you trust me? Do you not know our flocks are at war?"

TRYST

Ibn insisted.

"Satan is at war with God's creation. The fact that many men have become his pawns, men of all factions to one degree or another, does not make them the enemy. Besides, I have seen your heart—and aside from understandable interior struggles, it is pure."

Ibn felt momentarily exposed, knowing the Pontiff's notorious reputation for being able to read souls. Yet at the same time, he could not deny feeling a sense of affirmation at the holy man's discerned conclusion. He bowed his head, placing his hand over his heart. "As Allah wills."

The first vestiges of Easter sunlight began to materialize from the east as several hundred men, leaders of the many Christian traditions and communities, emerged from three days of intense prayer and fasting. Though instead of solemn and drawn faces, as would be the case for those who lacked sleep and food, their countenances beamed with joy, only tempered by a touch of resoluteness. All began the half-kilometer trek to the cathedral.

The final five to emerge from the structure were Hanoch Moss, Eliot Lige, Peter, Andreas, and a dazed Ibn Fatimah. As the others breathed deeply of the Mediterranean air, Ibn softly spoke his first words in three days.

"I thank you for your hospitality." He seemed to struggle to find words. "There is much that I must take to prayer. The ways of Allah can be quite... *mysterious*." He turned to Eliot. "I expect that I will remain here for some time, but eventually, I will have to return. I do not know if the Caliph believes me alive or dead. But I do sense, Mr. Lige, that our paths will cross once again." With that, Ibn bowed and departed in the opposite direction of the throng.

Eliot looked back to Peter. "A Bride united is a force to be reckoned with in these latter days, Holy Father."

Peter nodded but seemed to be clutched by a distant thought. They began to walk along the road to the cathedral as Peter continued to gaze out across the Mediterranean Sea. Without averting his gaze, he spoke. "So all the Elect have been counted and marked?"

Hanoch responded. "Yes, Holy Father, with those who were with us these days, now counted."

With that, Peter stopped and looked back to his three friends. He locked eyes with Andreas momentarily, after which the Patriarch nodded solemnly. Peter's eyes, now reflecting a spark of Divine Revelation, fell upon Eliot and Hanoch.

"These Elect must now go forth to the most remote regions of the Earth, proclaiming Christ crucified. Not one soul must have the Divine invitation withheld. They will be persecuted, but not harmed, for this is their time... the time of the New, and Final, Evangelization of the age. This must all come to pass before *The Gathering*."

"And what of our people, Holy Father? What of the Jews?"

Peter's eyes again met those of Andreas before returning to Eliot and Hanoch. "After *The Gathering*, the salvation of the Jews will be at hand. You two, alone will be the Lord's witnesses to His chosen people."

A silent spirit of approbation pierced the hearts of all present. Peter spoke again, this time in a much more solemn tone. "My time grows short. There is one more task God asks from me. Yet I cannot escape the sense that all is not as it should be."

Eliot was dumbfounded. "Most Holy Father, do not say—"

But Peter raised his hand. "Please, my brothers, for it is for you to witness the crucible to come, once I have fallen." Then looking directly at Hanoch and Eliot, he spoke with clear resolution. "You shall seek out the *Smited One*, and it will be the three of you who will lead the Remnant, as the Elect will be among you no more."

Peter looked down again to Andreas, who could not pull his eyes from the throng, which now began to enter the cathedral for a celebration of the Holy Sacrifice of the Mass. This Mass would be like none other celebrated in the past millennia. His eyes filled with tears, and despite his growing infirmity, the words which escaped from his lips were as crisp as the first morning which heralds the arrival of the new springtime.

"Forgiveness is a Divine gift. Today, we celebrate the resurrection of our Lord. Yet come nightfall, the time for penance will be at hand."

9

But then a great darkness covered the theater of all existence, as it came to be known that, though the Spiritual Entity was infinite and divine, the Physical Entity was finite, and as such, possessed a limited era of existence.

And it came to pass that the Spiritual Entity, which wished to honor the existence of the Physical Entity, accepted the responsibility of absorbing its essence into the *Kôles*. In this manner, though the Physical Entity would be no more, her substance finally decaying into nothingness, its essence would still live on in the *Kôles*.

And so it happened that the Spiritual Entity further extended herself into each life form in the physical world, grasping what salvageable essence she could, then returning to the *Kôles* at the end of the cycle of each life form. With the completion of each lifecycle, the *Kôles* assimilated a greater portion of the essence of the Physical Entity into herself.

Leviat F: 11-15
Book of Given Truths

i

It was early morning on their second week of traveling. Simon and Nathan had agreed that it would be unwise to head directly for Vannie Storm's home, as their pursuers would likely look there first. Even so, they themselves were not confident they could find the location. Traveling without the aid of the *i-Nav's* GPS and Signage System (a video screen which essentially substituted for most road signs), they were nearly driving blind, as fewer and fewer traditional street signs remained.

Simon was exhausted, never allowing Nathan to take his hand at the wheel for reasons he chose not to elaborate on. As he came upon an exit that identified the presence of lodging, he pulled the vehicle off the highway and onto a back road.

Nathan woke from his light sleep and looked towards Simon as he stretched. "What gives?"

Simon only half-glanced in Nathan's direction. "I'm just tired," he responded. "Thought we might hole up in another out-of-the-way town for a day or so."

Nathan shrugged his shoulders and wiped the last bit of sleep from his eyes. He looked up to read a street sign on the edge of the road as the car passed it.

Sardis 8 Kilometers

Nathan did not give much notice to the marking on the sign next to the name Sardis, which resembled a sort of cursive "C".

Within ten minutes, the two entered the small town. Nathan felt a strange sensation within him—one which he could not readily identify, except that he was… *unsettled*. Simon, his mind on a totally different track, spoke up.

"Now isn't this something?"

Nathan looked up, quickly becoming aware that the people walking along the sidewalks all smiled and waved to them as they approached. As soon as they passed by them, Nathan noticed that the people just went about their previous business. As they continued to scan the scene, Nathan and Simon realized that *all* the townsfolk were smiling.

"It's obviously another retro-town." Simon mused, now noticeably a bit uncomfortable himself.

"Retro-town?"

Simon nodded. "Yeah, there are literally thousands of them. When the economy completely tanked, it was hard on everyone… well… I know you remember that. But when prosperity began to return a couple years ago, and return with a vengeance, many towns rejected it. They had adapted to a much simpler and austere way of life."

"Then what's with the stupid smiles on their faces?"

Simon shook his head. "Damned if I know, that's new to me. Kind of creepy, isn't it?"

Nathan nodded, still mystified and admittedly a bit spooked by the scene. Simon pulled the car into a parking space in front of what looked to be a motel. They stepped out of the vehicle just as an old man walked by them, still moving rather gracefully for a man his age.

"Good day, my brothers! Welcome to Sardis," he said with a smile and a slight nod of his head, then continued on his way.

A discoloration on the man's hand caught Nathan's eye, but he was unable to fully make it out. Simon and Nathan exchanged mildly amused glances and walked into the motel.

They approached the front desk, where a woman, probably in her thirties, looked up to them with a pleasant smile.

"Good day, my brothers! Welcome to Sardis!"

Simon and Nathan were again about to exchange looks but both thought better of it. "Good day," Simon remarked politely.

He began to discuss arrangements for accommodations with the woman, but Nathan had tuned both of them out when he saw the marking on the back of the woman's right hand. It *was* a sort of discoloration, but definitely manmade. It most closely resembled the shape of a "C". Nathan had no doubt that it was also what the old man had on his hand. Though he could not put his finger on it, the marking seemed vaguely familiar.

"What's that marking on your hand?" Nathan asked, now realizing he had just interrupted the two.

The woman's smile returned. "That is called the Seal, it identifies us among the Saved, though it is really ourselves who do the saving."

"The Saved?" Simon inquired with a hint of a scowl.

"Why yes. We have chosen to follow the ways of the Spiritual Entity and to pursue reintegration with the *Kôles. The Way* is the means by which we learn of—"

"The Way?" Nathan interrupted. "You mean you're like some sort of Christian cult or something?"

An astonished look came across the woman's face. "Oh no, my brother! Oh no, not at all! I speak of the *true* Way, The Way of Mystic Realism."

Nathan could not fully restrain himself, glancing at Simon with an expression of mild amusement.

The woman continued, seemingly unfazed by their obvious skepticism. "I can see that you are not familiar with the teachings of the Great Prophet Tæsír Hoc, which is not a crime by any means. But I would like to offer you the opportunity to understand what is actually taking place in the physical world."

The woman reached underneath her counter and pulled out a red book. The front was embossed with gold lettering which read **Lib Dône Verü** *Book of Given Truths.*

Nathan immediately raised his hands in a gesture signaling that he was not interested. "No, thank you, ma'am, I'm not into this religious stuff." He chuckled lightly. "There seems to have been a devil in my life since I can remember, but never any god."

The woman nodded affirmatively with mild compassion, yet void of any hint of pity. "I can understand what you are saying, my brother. The *Ďishaläk* have blocked you from true comprehension. But please understand that, although it is called The Way, Mystic Realism is not a religion. It is more a transcendent philosophy based on social truths and reality itself." The woman released her smile, briefly, replacing it with more of a matter-of-fact look. "But please, don't take my word for it, take the Book, and your stay here is on the house." As she said the word 'house', the woman slid a room key onto the counter.

Nathan was about to politely refuse the offer when Simon reached over for the book, placing it in Nathan's hands, then he snatched up the key. "Thank you very much, ma'am... ahh... sister. We're cool with that!"

With that Simon tugged at Nathan's shirttail, and the two moved towards the stairs to their room.

ii

Siro was floating.

He found himself perhaps a meter above the floor in some strange hospital. The sensation was not altogether unpleasant, yet still unfamiliar. A moment passed, and then he felt himself descending, his feet gently touched the floor. The momentary tranquility was interrupted when, from behind a set of double doors, a woman screamed.

Siro moved, apprehensively at first, towards the doors. He realized he could now hear the unmistakable sound of a baby crying as well. He opened the door and found...

A doctor trembling on his knees, his head buried in his hands, crying. The mother gazed upwards, gasping for what Siro somehow knew to be her last breaths. Then, from around the back of the bed, out of the deepest depths of hell, crawled a newborn baby whose eyes glowed blood red. A light smoke began to rise from the infant's forehead, growing thicker and thicker as a sizzling sound sent shivers through Siro's entire body. Siro's eyes widened as he witnessed the Seal emerge from the baby's forehead.

A slight grin came across the child's face, as its mouth opened mechanically:

"Better make that deadline, Brother Siro."

Siro jumped up with a start from the place where he sat. For a moment, he had no idea where he was. His orientation quickly returning, the senior editor-in-chief realized he was sitting in front of his word processor.

He never had been one to have nightmares. Worse yet, he had never been one to fall asleep on the job. But recently he had begun to feel lethargic more often than not, and the dreams now came nearly every night... sometimes even in the middle of the day.

He had to get this article out, announcing Jimi T.'s first selection into his new band. Jimi T. had chosen none other than J.J. Hambon of *Saber-Tooth* for his new group. Hambon was arguably the greatest drummer in the world, and had recently declared his allegiance to The Way of Mystic Realism.

The announcement would coincide with Billboard's publication identifying *Something Borrowed* as the number one album in the world. Each person who purchased the album would automatically become a subscriber to the semi-weekly publication *The Signs of the Times*, joining the one hundred fifty million other readers across the world, which was now translated into seventeen different languages.

Despite lapses such as he had just experienced, these days Siro found himself expanding his repertoire of techniques to get a good story. A slight amount of encouragement here, a few calls with just the right amount of intimidation there, and, of course, the almighty (and newly invigorated) dollar had opened up a whole new world for him.

He reached over for the joint he had rolled, laced with just a touch of L.S.D., and lit it. Siro inhaled deeply and slowly let his breath out. This was a new vice for him, but a pleasant one, and one which would relax and promote the flow of the Life-Force through him, bringing him closer to the *Kôles*.

This was going to be good...

iii

"Let us then listen to the words of the Great Teacher Sammaet, in his Testament, verse T:1-5."

Tæsír Hoc walked behind the circle of two-dozen or so aspiring businessmen, each sitting cross-legged on the floor, turning the pages in their *Book of Given Truths* to the Testament of Sammaet.

"And I speak through my brothers: 'And in those latter days, the Spirit of the Life-Force will return to the world of matter in song. And it will be this melody that becomes a beacon to those who have grown less connected, and serves as a bond for those who have been true to the essence of the Spiritual Entity.'"

Each individual present, realizing that the Great Teacher had momentarily paused, gazed up at the Tæsír, their eyes and ears yearning for more. The Prophet held out his hands, and each participant subsequently raised their right hands, the Seal glowing slightly.

The Tæsír continued. "The Spirit of the Life-Force is among us, my brothers and sisters, and take heed of his song, for it is the words that tickle our minds, the verse which touches our hearts, but it is the *music* that encompasses our souls."

He looked down upon all of them, closing the book.

"Find the point where the three join, and you shall find eternal destiny!"

10

PATMOS – In a not unexpected address by Pope Peter II yesterday, the pontiff announced the Catholic Church's unequivocal condemnation of *The Way of Mystic Realism* and its proponents. It is anticipated that several other countries under the spiritual control of the Pope will follow suit.

The Pontiff described the movement as "a Godless cult inspired by Satan himself... fully incompatible with the Gospel". All artifacts of *The Way*, including the sacred *Book of Given Truths* have been banned from all property owned by the Catholic Church and its subsidiaries, and Catholics around the globe are being denied the right to possess any items related to *The Way*, including recordings made by Mystic Realism's favorite son, Jimi T. Expo.

In an unrelated story, Italian officials are looking into some undisclosed allegations made against Peter II while he was a parish priest in Rome, then known as Father Pietro Columba. No further information has been provided on this matter.

i

Simon entered the room with the takeout food he and Nathan had ordered. He took a brief moment to go through the bag he had grabbed from the ceramic jar before he and Nathan had escaped from his home.

Good ol' Uncle Garf. How did you know?

The bag was filled with pre-paid currency cards, untraceable to their purchaser. His government-fearing uncle had insisted he keep a stash "for an emergency."

"A cashless society," Uncle Garf had instructed, *"is the final step in the total dependence of each citizen on the government."*

Simon had thought his beloved uncle a paranoid nut at the time. But considering their circumstances, it seemed the man was a true freethinker. At the same time, it would seem his uncle had not foreseen the emergence of retro-towns; it took Simon three eating establishments before he could find one which offered a credit card machine.

He stepped back from the closet area, and then an overdone look of amazement came across his face as he saw that Nathan was breezing through the book the woman had given them.

"Nathan, I'm shocked, you can… *read?*"

Nathan looked up at his friend with a disapproving smirk. "Very funny, Wilson. This is how these pathetic cults work, they bore you to death until you have no choice but to listen!"

Simon smiled to himself as he began to set the food out. He opened his bottle of tonic water and sat down by the desk.

Nathan continued. "Do you know there are only two television stations that come in at this place? One is this freak called Tessie Hack, or something like that, talking about this Mystic Realism thing, and the other is a music video station, but it seems to play Jimi T. Expo almost exclusively—the bastard!"

Simon handed Nathan his sandwich and drink, then plopped down in the chair across from him. "So what do you think about the book?"

Nathan shrugged his shoulders. "To be honest, it's not as bad as I thought. It's kind of strange. I threw it down on the bed when we got here, and it fell open to a page. A few hours later, when I picked it up, a verse on that page caught my eye."

Simon looked at Nathan, seeming only mildly interested.

"Well," Nathan continued, determined to share this point with Simon whether he liked it or not, flipping through the book and until he found his place. "It was written by this guy called 'Naamak'. Anyway, it says, and I quote, 'Music is the vessel through which we achieve divine truth and wisdom.' Pretty good, huh? It's about time some religion realized the power of music. I could really get into that!"

Simon smiled lightly, munching away at the sandwich he had bought. He switched on the television, and sure enough, another Jimi T. Expo video came on.

"See what I mean?" Nathan said, pointing, with a mouthful of food. "Only, the moron's not actually *in* any of the videos... that makes a lot of frikkin' sense!"

"Easy there, big guy," Simon replied. "I'm detecting just the slightest bit of jealousy here." And then with a slight smirk he said, "I'm sure your precious book has something to say about that too."

And without releasing his smile, Simon ducked quickly to his right, avoiding the copy of the *Book of Given Truths* which sailed swiftly through the air past his head, hitting the closet door.

ii

Tæsír Hoc sat cross-legged on the floor. Completing the circle with him sat a dozen men, each distinguished in appearance, yet adorned in simple, light gray robes. An unlit candle rested in front of each individual, next to which sat a copy of the *Book of Given Truths*.

"Let us join," the Prophet commanded, and the group obliged him by joining hands.

"We have in this room," he continued, "the future leaders of the Western world, men called by the very Spiritual Entity herself. Let us open ourselves to her power. Let us shed the archaic skin of religious doctrine, so that we may open ourselves to the flow to the *Kôles*."

The Prophet closed his eyes, as did the rest of the men. A warm breeze swept through the room. He opened his eyes and began speaking in a mystical tone.

"It is written that, when all life becomes in tune with the *Kôles*, one collective conscious will come into existence, from which the human subsistence will evolve into a higher plane; this existence will merge the world of thought and the essence of flesh into one."

He paused, savoring the power which gave him his being.

"Now, my brothers, open your eyes and witness the power of the Life-Force!"

They did so, and immediately the candles sprung to life, a bright flame burning atop each.

"More," the Prophet beckoned.

And the flames grew larger.

"MORE!" he commanded.

The flames grew larger and more intense as the light in the room became unbearably bright. The temperature began to rise, and a low rumble filled the room. The Tæsír's eyes burned with fire.

"Open yourselves now, my brothers! Give yourself to the Life-Force, and you shall not burn!"

At that moment, the tapestries on the walls began to catch fire. A paradoxical darkened 'light' came forth, as sweat began to drip profusely from each man's face. At that moment, one of the members of the group screamed out in panic, immediately bursting into flames.

"DO NOT RELEASE THE BOND!" the Prophet called out, and the others held tightly to the hands of the man as he, now fully engulfed in flames, continued to scream.

And in a flash, it was over. The light died down, as did the temperature. The floor was covered with a light film of wax. The group released hands, following suit with the Prophet. They each, albeit reluctantly, looked towards the pile of ashes where the one man had sat.

"The Spirit has spoken, and we must keep ourselves on guard at all times. Today we had an Infector among us, and today is also the last day that he will attempt to pollute the *Kôles*."

The Prophet looked around the room, meeting eyes with each member present. He finally rested his gaze upon one man. "Brother William, step forth."

William Maison rose as instructed, moved across the circle, and then knelt before the Prophet. The two joined hands and bowed their heads. Tæsír Hoc spoke.

"It has been revealed to me that you will be the first from The Way of Mystic Realism to lead in the Western world. Do you accept your commission?"

Maison raised his head, meeting the Prophet's eyes. "I do, Great Teacher."

Tæsír Hoc smiled. "Then go forth, my brother, preach the truth, and serve the Spirit of the *Kôles*!"

iii

Kenny Lydon sat in his car a half-kilometer from Vanya Ciotola's home, well out of sight. This was the nineteenth day he would wait at the same spot; waiting for Nathan Freeman to show up, which he was sure would never happen. Lydon got on the two-way radio.

"This is K.L., over."

"Go ahead, K.L."

He paused momentarily, then pressed the speak button. "Listen, Jake, this is a bust. Nesterov's still staying with her, and the place is crawling with his men. If this Freeman guy's got two brain cells, he won't show within a thousand kilometers of the place."

Hanssen's voice cracked back. "Unless they're working together, then he'd go straight here."

Lydon shook his head, took another look through his binoculars as he released the transmitter. He knew Jake Hanssen's only chance to get his sentence fully rescinded was to establish a link between the Freeman kid and Nesterov. He also knew Hanssen's time was limited. In another nine days, he would be seen before the judge again. And this time, no fancy lawyer would be able to get him off.

Unless…

DOMINION

iv

Somewhere, a thousand kilometers away, a young woman lost her faith.

11

> "It was at this time that I heard the third trumpet blast, and I saw before me a great field which stretched off into eternity. Upon the field, I saw three times twelve herds of sheep, separated from each other, yet grazing among their closest kindred. A scattered number of goats roamed in and out of the herds, sometimes taking several sheep with them to the others. Then I heard a great voice call from the Heavens like the sound of a lion's roar, 'Who hath dispersed My flock?' I looked up to see a great Shepherd, clothed in brilliant light, come forth from a faraway land. He raised his staff, and the many herds of sheep joined and became one. Yet the goats He did not call forth, for they were not of his flock."

– St. Vincent of the Sand (967-996)

i

Simon and Nathan drove out of Sardis after a bizarre, but not altogether disagreeable, three-day stay. Both had found the town to be, despite all the weirdness, peaceful. Nathan found himself having to admit that an entire community with the same religion and philosophy definitely had its benefits.

Simon had spent most of his time in Sardis sleeping, while Nathan surprised even himself by reading a good portion of the *Book of Given Truths*.

"They'll make a holy roller out of you yet, Nathan!" Simon had joked. Nathan, of course, did not appreciate this implication at all, almost halting his reading because it gave Simon some odd sort of satisfaction. He was *not* "studying" a religious philosophy. He simply found the book, and its point of view, intriguing.

Simon drove the car, as Nathan continued to read. Being in a retro-town had additional benefits for their cause; they found a road map—a mostly extinct concept today—at the front desk during checkout.

As they continued to drive towards their destiny, Nathan perpetuated a ritual which he had developed back in Sardis with Simon.

"This is wild, Simon," he began, Simon already preparing himself for what was about to come. "It describes religion as no more than an archaic system which was developed to provide structure for our evolution. Almost like it had a purpose, I guess to organize us and give us a reason not to kill each other off before we even got started."

"You don't say," Simon responded, only mildly interested.

"Yeah," Nathan continued. "It was a needed step in the evolution of the human race. It says we used to need a reason... a *divine* reason, to be good to each other because the tangible world is naturally self-serving, and not naturally just."

"I suppose that makes sense, Mr. Philosopher."

"Screw you. Anyway, now that we've learned the social benefits of working together, we don't need this religion garbage anymore. We've learned that treating each other right is best for everybody in the long run, and we don't need a deity to tell us that."

"So are you gonna convert, Nathan?"

Nathan looked up from his book to Simon. *"From what?"*

A wide grin broke out across Simon's face. "Oops, my mistake. I forgot that you're a non-denominational atheist."

"I'm nothing, Simon, it's that simple. I'm just enjoying the concepts I'm reading—kind of like Dianetics or something."

"Dude, I hope not."

TRYST

Nathan looked inquisitively at his friend. He hesitated for a moment, then decided to speak. "Hey, Simon, are *you* in any sort of religion? I guess I've never asked before."

Simon raised an eyebrow slightly. "I suppose. My parents, hell, my entire family is composed of a bunch of Hasidic Jews."

Nathan looked at Simon, astonished. "You're a *Jew*?"

Simon chuckled. "Worse than that my friend, a *Hasidic* Jew. You know, ultra-conservative, if something feels good, it's a sin. The whole nine yards."

"I had no idea."

"How could you?" Simon asked rhetorically. "I guess I've kind of fallen under the Jewish form of excommunication—me and Uncle Garf, that is."

He stopped, not offering any additional information un-prodded, but Nathan was too intrigued not to pursue this topic further. "So what happened?"

Simon hesitated, wondering if he really wanted to get into all this. After mulling it over momentarily, he decided to proceed. "Well, you know part of it. I slipped up a bit, became an alcoholic and a drug addict, which, by the way, were not considered behaviors becoming of a Hasidic Jew."

"Damn!"

"Yep, life's a bowl of cherries, huh? Anyway, I was eventually kicked out of the house, spent four years wandering in hell, then finally kicked the habit. And the rest, as they say—"

"Wait a minute," Nathan interrupted "I knew you were a user, but I never learned how you were able to stop. How *did* you kick such a bad habit?"

Simon sighed. "Well, I guess Narcotics Anonymous was a big part of it, but the truth is, I found a new addiction."

"Which was?"

"Music—classical primarily. It became everything for me. It filled the void I was feeling at the time. A void which I guess I had had my whole life."

Nathan watched as Simon's eyes slowly moved towards his artificial limb. A look of sadness rested in his gaze as an awkward silence set in.

"You know," Nathan began, "there are a lot of ways you can still make music. You don't have to have two h—"

"That night, Nathan," Simon angrily cut in. "That one bitch of a night, I lost *everything* that was important to me. I lost my friend, I lost the chance to do something right, and I lost my FUCKING HAND!"

Nathan was speechless as he witnessed a side of Simon he had never seen. He pretended not to notice the lone tear that slid down the side of Simon's cheek.

"And with all that," Simon continued, his voice now subdued, "went my passion for music... as if it never were there to begin with."

Nathan chose not to speak at this point, not knowing what exactly he should, or could, say. He could not help but think, however, of a phrase he had just come across in the *Book of Given Truths*.

'Nature abhors a vacuum.'

And he pondered, silently, what had, or would, fill that void which pained his friend so.

ii

Jimi T. Expo stood on the balcony of his mansion overlooking the Pacific Ocean. He watched the stars gleam down upon the waters as a mystical tune quietly arose from his lips. Tæsír Hoc approached from behind him.

"Your Lordship?"

Without moving, Jimi T. responded. "Yes, dear *Hocus Pocus*, do approach."

Hoc grimaced as he stepped forward. "It's *Tæsír H—*"

"Yes, yes, as you say. What news do you bring me?"

The Prophet clenched his teeth, not having grown used to having a superior to answer to upon this Earth. "I understand you have selected a second—"

Jimi T. nodded and turned towards him. "Yes, yes, I have. I have chosen Keith Entwire, the bassist and backing vocalist for *Arameaus*."

Hoc looked away, trying to mask his disgust. Jimi T. spoke again.

"Do not waste your energy trying to cover your displeasure from me. Your time as *my* teacher has ended, for I have nothing left to learn from you. I grow weary of your non-acceptance of this truth."

Hoc looked down. "I understand this, Your Lordship, yet I cannot help but think that you are—"

"The moment I took this form, I ceased being... *that*." Though Jimi T. maintained a firm and unwavering tone, it was devoid of emotion. "Accept your destiny, your *role*, or I *will* find another. Is that clear, *Sir Pocus*?"

Hoc held back an interior storm, speaking through clenched teeth. "Very clear, Your Lordship."

"Your worthless emotions betray your words and sicken me in their weakness. It does not please the Master."

Jimi T. turned again towards the waters. He waited a moment before speaking again. "Is Nathaniel Freeman en route?"

Hoc, regathering his sense of respectability, spoke. "He is coming to you, Your Lordship. I can feel it."

"As do I."

"But," Hoc continued, "I cannot help but ask why it is that you have chosen him; he is not one of us, he is—"

"Must I remind you, dear *Hocus*, that it is not for you to ask, and it is not for me to explain to you. Mr. Freeman is part of the greater plan, and in time, he will serve the Master. But for now, it will be me that he serves..."

iii

"This whole thing really smells like a *perdet'*, Felix," Nesterov asserted.

Felix Amosov nodded as he spit out his overused nicotine gum from Vanya's porch. "I know, Alex, but for right now, we do not have much of a choice. They have Jeffrey Chardin's remains with a bullet in his skull, and a marriage license with Marisha's name on it. I suppose you owning the property does not help much either. You are an easy target for a suspect, but they will not be able to prove *govno*."

"But that was more than fifteen years ago! Is there not some sort of statute of limitations or something?"

"Not for murder, Alex," Amosov responded. "Look, it is just questioning, I am telling you. They do not have... how do they say? 'A snowball's chance in hell?'"

Nesterov thought for a moment, then nodded his head. "Okay, we will go through with it. How far is this place from here?"

"About two hours, give or take."

Nesterov nodded in acknowledgment. "Fine, we will go there tonight, stay for a day, no more than two, then get back here and get down to business."

Both Amosov and Nesterov stood. "And what about Vanya, Alex?"

Nesterov thought for a moment. "Any sign of those FBI guys watching us anymore?"

Amosov shook his head. "They gave up whatever wild goose chase they were on over a week ago."

"Is Andrey back yet?"

"He should be back later this evening. He had to teach his heavy-handed son-in-law-to-be a little lesson in the proper treatment of a lady."

Nesterov shook his head. "The stupid *svoloch'*. A man with an anger problem should not choose the last living daughter of Andrey Gavrilenkov for a wife."

"Sascha has not married him yet. Perhaps she will make a better decision."

"Perhaps she will. Russian women can be stubborn, but they are no match for the Irish." No sooner had the words left his lips than Nesterov suddenly looked down, his own sad reality kicking in. Amosov began to grapple for words in order to change the subject, but Nesterov beat him to the punch. "I believe two men should be fine in the meantime here. Perhaps Radchikov and Dostoevsky. Vanya seems to be doing better. Let us go and get this… what do they say here? 'horse and pony show' over with."

iv

Carl Woodward stepped into the office of Siro Scribner. It had been a whirlwind three weeks since he had joined the staff of *The Signs of the Times*. It was truly a dream for him; the opportunity right out of a graduate program to be an "insider" working for a news service that covered the most important issues of our time—all through the clear (and certainly true) perspective of Mystic Realism.

But when a strange and seemingly chance tryst left him with an anonymously-authored document in his hands, Carl had no idea where this could take him, but it led right to here; a meeting with the editor-in-chief of *The Signs of the Times*.

"Well hello! Come in, Brother Carl."

Siro was quite intrigued when he received news of what Carl had come across. They exchanged greetings, and Carl was momentarily captivated as he looked out at the breathtaking view from the senior editor-in-chief's office. Siro glanced up, quickly picking up on what his subordinate was thinking.

"Amazing, isn't it? Did you know, this building is built right on ground-zero of the dirty bomb set off fifteen years ago?"

Carl nodded. "I thought I had heard something to that effect. So there is no memorial?"

Siro shook his head, frowning. "Absolutely not. What good would a memorial do humanity, other than a reminder of the dangers of an archaic religion? Moving forward, progress and evolution, a much better way to combat religionists."

Carl again nodded. It made sense, and as he quickly discovered, pretty much *everything* made more sense when approached through the lens of Mystic Realism. Intellectual stimulation, without the superstition and repressive so-called "moral code" of the many dying religions. *True* liberty, *true* equality, *true* fraternity.

Life is good!

"So tell me," Siro began. "I understand you have come across some interesting information."

"Yes, I have. Really curious stuff. It involves a meeting."

"Yes?" Siro leaned forward.

"Yes, and it's funny that you mentioned the dirty-bomb incident because it allegedly took place a few weeks after that event, and it seems even *because* of it, on Hyde Island in Maine."

Siro nodded intently, gesturing for Carl to continue.

"Well, the guest list is quite impressive. Probably half were heads of big international business and news corporations, most of the rest were high-up government officials, and then it even had a number of foreign nationals. Seventy-two people in all."

"And who called the meeting?"

"Well, that's where it gets even more interesting. The meeting was headed by Elihu K. Maison."

"Maison?"

"Yes, the father of Senator William Maison. An interesting character in his own right. Almost no one knows about him, and he has, relatively speaking, very little personal money to his name. But behind the scenes, it seems he has control over hundreds of billions of dollars... perhaps even more."

"So I'm guessing that President Amarab was in on this 'secret meeting'?"

Carl shook his head. "Interestingly enough, he was not. He only had eighteen months left in his third term, and if you remember, he was blamed for the incident because of his longstanding policy of appeasement. Since he was unsuccessful in his attempts to frame it as being the result of religionists, he was probably considered a non-player by that time. But it seems that many of his Cabinet members *were* there. Members of both the Republican and Democratic Parties were present, though it seems like it was primarily filled with individuals who are now members of the Independence Party. The list even indicates Vlad Ivankov might have been present, though his name was marked through."

"Ohhh, the great Russian crime boss of our time, sounds like a conspiracy," Siro whispered with a wink.

Carl was a little perplexed by Siro's intonation, but continued.

"Well, yes, I would say."

"So what was the gist... the purpose of the meeting?"

"Well, more or less, it was to develop and advocate a twelve-year plan for the United States, and I guess in a sense, for the world."

Siro again frowned. "The 'New Independence Plan?' That's no secret."

"No," Carl continued, "not the *public* twelve-year plan, a different, underlying agenda. As crazy as it sounds, my source says they decided to *orchestrate* the U.S. economic collapse—the Second Depression—which of course did happen a few weeks later when OPEC froze all oil shipments to the U.S. and began trading on the Yen. These people wanted to promote a period of isolationism—which again, is what we have only started to emerge from in the past three years. But the 'end game' according to my source was to then re-emerge as a more socialist, less sovereign state."

Siro looked as if he was quickly growing impatient with this discussion.

This is ancient history, buddy. We now have the truth before us. Everything has changed.

Still, some part of the old journalist in him was interested enough to pursue this—at least for the duration of this meeting.

"That seems counterintuitive," Siro breathed. "If you wanted a more socialist and less sovereign nation, then the isolationist nationalism they promoted makes no sense. It's the polar opposite."

Carl nodded in a conciliatory fashion. "You would think that, but my source tells me that their belief was that a backlash against the isolationism could be nurtured, a very strong pendulum swing if you will. Their plan was to put a president in place that would be a strong isolationist—well, at least publicly. And of course, J.P. Warburg of the Independence Party was elected the following year."

"Well, yes, he was quite a strong nationalist, but our current president—Warburg's vice president for his first team—seems quite different."

"Yes, Hugh Lang didn't run with him for his second term, and in a subtle fashion became quite a critic of the administration, though he didn't formally leave the party for another year or so. He seems to be the trump card in all of this—"

"Trump card?" Siro cut in, starting to perceive many holes in this plot, "...or invalidator of this whole conspiracy theory? With our recent hyper-prosperity, and Lang's reaching out to other countries while still being a hard-liner on national sovereignty. It doesn't fit, the whole theory crumbles."

Carl acquiesced, a little. "Yes, it's going to be hard to have the intended backlash—the pendulum swing—if you will, when things are improving so rapidly under the current regime. Lang seems to be inadvertently undermining the plan."

"If there ever was a plan."

Carl only hesitated momentarily, grappling with an additional thought. "But even so, don't you find it interesting that President Lang filled his Cabinet and other high-ranking positions with complete outsiders—so to speak?"

"What do you mean by 'outsiders'?"

"Well, it has been pretty much the standard to fill the majority of these positions with members of the Triune Commission or the Concilium on Foreign Affairs. He doesn't have a single member of either entity in any of the high-power positions."

Siro sat back, trying to maintain an expression of serene skepticism, but he was unsure if he was successful at hiding the growing anxiety inside of him.

"Brother Carl, do you have the list?"

"The list?"

"Yes, of the attendees?"

"Why, yes."

"Can I see it?"

Carl Woodward was suddenly beginning to feel a bit uncomfortable. It was a legitimate request; why was he all of a sudden feeling protective?

"Why... ahh... sure," he stammered as he filed through his folder and pulled it out, handing it to Siro.

Siro quickly scanned the list and felt his heart begin to race. He looked up at the young—and no doubt naïve—journalist, again trying to feign a slight sense of intrigue, but not too much. Without returning the list, Siro spoke, now in a more assertive, authoritative tone.

"I desire our news service to be one that does not in any way reflect a tabloid. I need more corroborating information before we move forward with this, and I need to know your source."

Carl was stunned. "My source?"

Siro shook his head in disgust. "Please don't give me any of that 'protecting my source' garbage, Brother Carl. We are not a traditional news service. If you haven't noticed, we are living in different times. We print the truth, we provide complete transparency, and we make damn sure it *is* the truth before we print it. You need to dig up more on this. Maybe there is something to it, maybe there isn't. But I won't move forward until we get more. Is that understood?"

"Yes, sir. Understood."

Carl stood up, and somewhat awkwardly shook Siro's hand. As he exited the office, Siro prayed that he did not notice the light layer of perspiration that had emerged over his entire body. A struggle began within Siro's mind, seeing on the list the names of several men who had helped move

TRYST

him into this much-coveted position, including the primary benefactor of this news service. He reached hesitantly for his phone, then dialed a number.

The receptionist answered politely, "Colonel Huis Bildeberger's office, may I help you?"

Siro quickly slammed down the phone.

… and the struggle ensued…

12

i

"I do not know about you, Pavel, but I sure am hungry."

Pavel Radchikov looked back at the one-hundred-and-forty-kilogram mammoth called Dmitri, trying to decide if he was up for an argument or not. Dmitri, in Pavel's estimation, had taken the syndicate's relationship with the Caputo family too far, having developed quite a taste for Italian cuisine—*all* of it.

"We cannot, Dmitri. It is two kilometers to the nearest food stop, and we have orders not to leave the old lady alone."

"Come on, Pavel, it is seven o'clock; I have not eaten since lunchtime." Dmitri thought for just a moment, feeling his glands salivate as thoughts of Stromboli danced in his head, then continued. "Nothing is going to happen to the old lady. The feds are gone, and Gavrilenkov will be here within the hour anyway. There is not a thing that is going to happen. We shoot on down to the sub shop and get back here in no more than fifteen minutes. What can happen in fifteen minutes?"

Pavel opened his mouth to protest, but felt his stomach growl at the very moment he tried to do so. He looked towards the house of Vanya Ciotola, mulling the situation over for a moment.

"Fifteen minutes?"

"No more, I swear on my good mother's grave."

"Your mother is still alive."

"All the more reason. She would not want her son to be hungry."

Pavel nodded reluctantly and started up the vehicle. He took one last brief glance at the house before beginning their exciting journey to King Solomon's Sub Shop.

ii

Simon pulled onto the gravel driveway and reached over with his artificial hand to shake his traveling companion awake.

"Up and at 'em, dude. We're here."

Nathan began wiping the sleep from his eyes. "Where?"

"At Jonathan's mother's home... finally."

Nathan sat up and felt an eerie chill pass through him as they pulled up to the house. No lights appeared to be on. Simon glanced at his watch, which read a few minutes after seven p.m.

"I can't imagine she's asleep this early," Simon stated. "What do you want to do, Nathan?"

Nathan pushed the door open and began getting out of the car. "I didn't come this far just to hang around the house. Besides, doing that could be hazardous to my health."

Simon was perplexed. "What do you mean by that?"

"Oh, nothing really," Nathan replied, walking across the gravel driveway and stepping onto the front porch. Simon shrugged his shoulders, got out of the vehicle, and walked towards the steps as Nathan rapped on the front door.

For a moment it seemed as if no one would answer. Nathan was about to knock again when a light came on. He heard footsteps move towards the door.

"Who is it?" a frightened voice inquired.

"Mrs. S., it's me, Nathan, Jonathan's friend. And I've got Simon Wilson with me, he—"

The door opened swiftly, and Nathan found himself face to face with a frail and frightened Mrs. Vannie Storm.

"Nathan..." she whispered, tears coming to her eyes. "Oh, Nathan, for the love of God, they said you were dead!"

"It's... ahh... it's good to see you."

The two embraced, and Mrs. Storm a.k.a. Vanya Ciotola brought both Nathan and Simon into the house.

Nathan and Simon sat at the kitchen table while Mrs. Storm prepared hot chocolate for them. Nathan had already sensed something different about her, but could not put his finger on it. She looked to have aged a dozen years since he had last seen her. The woman moved to the table with three mugs on a serving plate.

"It is so good to see you both. Jesse told me I'd be having visitors."

Nathan glanced curiously at Simon, then back at Mrs. Storm. "Who's Jesse, Mrs. S.?"

She looked at Nathan as if he had a second head attached. "Well, you two were only best friends for six years!"

Nathan was puzzled. "You mean, *Jonathan*, Mrs. S.?"

She shook her head. "No, no, no, it's Jesse, and he said that a pair in great danger would come to me. He surely meant you two. He said that once you located the third, then you..."

As Mrs. Storm continued to talk, Nathan suddenly felt like he had been hit by a ton of bricks. He recalled his dream—or perhaps *vision* was a better word for it—where he had visited an individual who called himself Jesse, bearing a striking resemblance to Jonathan.

"…and that he's suffering in the desert, at the hands of Satan himself, and he will not—"

"Mrs. S.," Nathan interrupted. "I'm not real sure why we came, other than the fact that we don't have any place else to go. Jonathan was my friend. I—"

"Jesse," she corrected again. "And he shared that I should not let you stay, and that I needed to let you know, Nathan, that you need to beware, for as you go, darkness travels with you."

Nathan looked to Simon for assistance, or perhaps some enlightenment as to what she meant, but Simon had none to offer. It had become obvious to both of them that Mrs. S. was no longer playing with a full deck, and that staying any longer would probably prove fruitless—perhaps even dangerous.

Nathan smiled gently and looked towards her. "We're going to have to get moving, Mrs. S. Thank you for the hospitality."

"I'll make sure to tell Jesse that you two stopped by next time he speaks to me."

Simon smiled uncomfortably and rose from the table along with Nathan. The two bid Mrs. Storm farewell and slid out the front door into the approaching night.

Simon and Nathan had not been gone five minutes when Vanya heard a sound from within the house. She froze in her seat as footsteps approached the room where she sat. Vanya looked up to see two silhouettes standing just outside the threshold of the light. The first stepped forward into full visibility, while the other waited behind in the darkness.

"Good evening, Mrs. Storm, or is it Mrs. Ciotola, or perhaps, Miss Nesterov?"

Vanya eyed the strange man suspiciously. He was clothed in an off-white cassock, and possessed a well-groomed, mid-length white beard and leathery skin. "H-How did you get in here?"

The man smiled. "I do not feel that is very important. In fact, it would definitely be a squandering of both your time and mine to dwell upon such a thing. All that matters now, Vanya, is that I am here. And I would like to ask you, if I may, Vanya, do you know who I am?"

Vanya looked closely, and a mild expression of recognition came across her face. "Y-yes. Yes, I do. You're that preacher I saw on TV, the one who hates Christians. They call you Tes... ahh... Tes..."

"A simple 'Great Teacher' will do. But perhaps you might wish to look a bit closer, maybe even a bit... *deeper*, Vaaaaaannnnyaaaaaa."

Her eyes widened tenfold, and she felt every hair on her body stand erect. "Oh no," she whispered, her voice reflecting a despairing terror. "Oh, God, please no!"

Tæsír Hoc produced a fittingly sinister smile. "Oh yes, it is I, Vanya. And I have brought you a surprise. I know you're the sentimental type, so I took the liberty of inviting an acquaintance of yours along for this little tryst of ours. You know, I've always been a sucker for family reunions—well, sort of, I suppose."

At that moment, the second figure emerged from the darkness, and Vanya felt her heart stop.

"Good evening, *Auntie*."

"No!" she shrieked. "Dear Jesus! No! No! IT CAN'T BE!"

iii

Carl Woodward moved through the multitudes of books in the vast federal library. Nowadays, technology had made printed collections such as these more into museums than places of study.

At least you don't need electricity and an Internet connection to read these! He mused.

He moved through the different sections, arriving at the subject location that had been agreed upon. He looked up to see the sign, "Ceramic and allied technologies."

Not knowing exactly what to do, Carl began to look at some of the book titles.

"This is a foolish thing you have done, young man," a barely audible voice spoke from behind the books.

Carl was startled at first, but was then able to see the aged eyes from the next aisle looking through the bookcase.

"Pick out a book, and start looking at it," the voice commanded.

Carl did as he was told, feeling his heart rate beginning to elevate.

"This was not part of the agreement."

Carl kept his eyes down as he responded. "I can't do anything with what you've shown me. There are too many questions and inconsistencies."

"Young Siro would not act on what you have shown him?"

Carl began to shake his head, then remembered that he was to give the appearance of not being in the conversation.

"No, no he would not. In fact, it was a very uncomfortable meeting. Besides being overly skeptical, he wanted me to reveal my source. That is unthinkable for a journalist."

There was a low grunt from behind the books. "It would be the grossest of understatements to state that this is... *disappointing*. I had high hopes for that boy. He showed much promise." The voice faltered, and Carl was able to sense a trace of sadness in it. "But it is clear now that the once scrupulous journalist has fallen prey to his own corrupted appetites. We are both in danger now."

"Why?"

"Because his news corp's silent benefactor is a player in this."

"I don't understand. Where did you get that list? How did you know about this secret meeting?"

There was a brief, but very clear, pause. "Because my name is on that list."

Carl felt the blood drain from his face. "You were part of this? Then why blow the whistle? Why now?"

"Can a dying old man rediscover his conscience?"

Carl stood there, recognizing that his ruse of reading a book was not working well. He placed one book back in as he selected another. He allowed another glance at the aged eyes through the bookshelf. He could see that they were filling.

"There must have been a reason."

The voice was steady. "Son, I have participated in many forms of evil in my life, but none as diabolical as this one. My great-grandfather was party to a similar meeting off the coast of South Carolina many years ago, and brought his own son—my grandfather—into its unholy circle. When my own aspirations for power became evident as a young man, my grandfather pulled me aside and tried to caution me of the dangerous path I was heading down. But of course, I would not listen. I have no sons or grandsons to warn, my mistresses were power, wealth, and the indulgence of these appetites."

"So why me?"

Carl thought he detected a slight chuckle from the other side.

"You have a uniquely interesting lineage, Mr. Woodward."

The comment sent many questions through Carl's head, but he suppressed them, as he knew his time was limited.

"Well, then I have only one part of this entire conspiracy theory that makes absolutely no sense."

"President Hugh Lang, I presume?"

"Yes, it just doesn't fly. In fact, it pretty much negates everything you've told me. If the goal was to have a strictly isolationist and nationalistic policy, and then deliberately cause it to fail so miserably so as to create such a backlash that our nation would gladly relinquish much of its sovereignty to international socialistic forces in exchange for prosperity, well, with everything Lang is doing right now—beginning to reach out to other countries, making unprecedented economic progress—the chances of this desired 'backlash' are diminishing by the day!"

There was another subtle chuckle, then the voice again spoke. "Perhaps God does have the final word."

"What?"

The pause at this point was so long that Carl looked up to see if his source was still there. He was, but his voice now changed to something much more urgent.

"Listen closely, Mr. Woodward, because this will be the last thing you will hear me say. These men do not think in years or even political cycles—they think in *generations*. Most of the world is either under their control or moving in that direction, but not everyone."

TRYST

The tone of the voice was now causing icy fingers to slither up through Carl's innards. The voice continued.

"Hugh is a boy scout—a true believer in the classic sense. He sees through this nonsense of phony politics and reconstituted evil wrapped in a prettier package, and he knows the plans of powerful men. After the death of his son during his term as vice president, he had a sort of conversion, you might say. And now with the remainder of his family gone, he truly is a man with nothing to lose. How he has lived through all these assassination attempts, I can only attribute to Divine intervention. But he will not see the end of his second term."

Attempts? There had only been one, but the latter part of the statement kept Carl from interrupting. There was again a pause, but Carl could practically taste the pain as the voice continued, now audibly trembling.

"…and I will not see the sunrise tomorrow."

Carl's head shot up. "What?"

The eyes were gone. Carl quickly sprinted to the end of the bookcases, then shot a glance down the next aisle. No one was there.

The man slid quickly out the back door of the library into the warm evening air. Despite his age, he maintained a quick pace as he moved in and out of alleyways, soon arriving at his final destination. He entered the doors of St. John the Apostle Catholic Church and hastened his way into the confessional. He fell to his knees and the screened casement opened.

"It's me," he said. "I have done what you required of me."

The familiar voice from the other side spoke. "Not what *I* have required, but God and your conscience. Your penance is fulfilled. You are a free man now, in the truest sense of the word."

The man's eyes filled with tears as he got up and exited the confessional. As he walked out the front doors of the church, he did not even notice Father Daniel Ananias step out of the confessional whispering, "Go in peace, your sins are forgiven."

The man took three paces down the church steps and came directly upon a familiar face from many years ago. He smiled gently as he made the Sign of the Cross, his fingers still damp from their brief dip in the holy water font just a moment before. His last breath on this Earth was given in deep gratitude to his Savior.

13

Allied Press ~

NEW YORK - In an announcement which has left many third-world countries in fear, the United Nations announced its dissolution yesterday.

To most world leaders, the announcement did not come as a surprise. Over the past twelve years, the U.N. has grown weaker and more obscure, fueled by continued dissension amongst its participants. Many attribute the dissolution to the body's inability effectively engage the crises in India and Africa.

In a statement released at a press conference yesterday, Secretary General Pan Obsolaat cited an "increasingly archaic body granted insufficient autonomy and power to cope with modern world problems…" as the reasons behind the decision to dissolve the entity.

No indication has been given as to a possible successor to this international body.

TRYST

i

Nathan and Simon lay face down in the gravel at the end of Mrs. Storm's driveway. Dmitri stood over them, one foot resting not so gently on the back of Nathan's neck, and holding a pistol at Simon's head.

"I am going to ask you one more time. What were you doing at Ms. Ciotola's house?"

"I told you," Nathan responded painfully. "We don't know any Ms. Ciotola. We were visiting our friend's mother, we—"

"This is a waste of time," Pavel stated, grateful that they had arrived before these two could pull any mischief. "I'm going to go up to the house and check on her. You keep these two guys covered. If either of them moves, waste them both."

"No problem, Pavel."

Pavel Radchikov started to walk briskly towards the house. Dmitri removed his foot from Nathan's neck and leaned down to get a better look at his face. "You know, kid, you really look familiar. Do I know you?"

Nathan's heart rate increased as he strained not to show any reaction to the mammoth's statement. His Russian accent was clear, these were Nesterov's men. "N-No, sir."

Pavel was about halfway to the house when an ear-piercing scream erupted from inside. Dmitri jerked his head in the direction of the commotion.

"DMITRI!" Pavel screamed out as he sprinted towards the house.

Dmitri looked down at Nathan and Simon, hesitating. At that instant, a black limousine pulled around the corner and onto the gravel driveway.

"*Chyort voz'mi*," Dmitri whispered to himself.

The limousine came to a stop out of necessity, being blocked by both Nathan and Simon's vehicle, as well as the one driven by Pavel and Dmitri.

The doors to the limousine jerked open, and Alexandre Nesterov, among others, stepped out with a perplexed look on his face.

Another scream rang out from inside the house as Pavel tried to kick in the front door, which had somehow become jammed shut. Dmitri and Nesterov met eyes for only a moment before Dmitri turned and sprinted towards the house.

Several more of Nesterov's men took off towards the house as did he. But Nesterov slowed for a moment, having caught a brief glance at the two young men getting up from in between the two vehicles.

Nathan and Nesterov's eyes met. It took only an instant for Nesterov to recall the face. His mouth fell agape. "Y-you? You are supposed to be…"

Nesterov did not bother finishing his sentence and drew his pistol from under his suit jacket. Nathan's eyes widened as both he and Simon dove for cover behind Dmitri's car. Nesterov fired a half-dozen rounds at them—the majority of which pierced the car—before a third scream emanated from the house.

Nesterov hesitated for a moment before moving his aging body towards the house, still firing in the direction of Nathan and Simon as he did so, cursing the parental figures that brought them into existence.

The screaming had ended. As his men swept the house, Nesterov, on his knees, held Vanya in his arms. Her hair had fallen out, and her pupils were such small specks that they may as well not have existed. She labored heavily to breathe.

"Oh, Vanya," Nesterov cried. "Oh God, not you, Vanya. Please God, no!"

Vanya attempted to swallow, but could not, and gagged. She looked up dreamily toward her father. Her lips began to move. Nesterov looked down as several of his tears dripped onto Vanya's face. He realized she was trying to say something to him.

Nesterov leaned down, bringing his ear up as close to her lips as he possibly could.

She struggled in between breaths, then whispered, "It was him, Papa… it was…" and breathed no more.

Nathan and Simon had sprinted for the woods without looking back. From behind, Simon could see blood dripping from the side of Nathan's head. After a solid fifteen minutes of running, they both collapsed behind a thick oak from exhaustion.

In between gasps, Simon spoke up. "Your head, man. Are you hit?"

Nathan looked at Simon, still trying to draw enough oxygen into his lungs to speak, then reached his hand up to his ear. When he looked at his hand it was covered in blood. "Must of... just... clipped me..." he managed to get out. He looked down at Simon, who was lying among the wet leaves. "How about you?"

Simon began to look himself over. "No, I—"

Nathan looked curiously at Simon as he abruptly stopped speaking. Simon was staring at his artificial hand.

"What is it?"

Simon looked up at Nathan with a slight grin on his face and held up his prosthetic. Nathan could see where a bullet had lodged in the center of it.

"Man of steel."

Nathan stared intently at the hand, then back to Simon, and a moment later two weeks of soul-piercing tension was released instantaneously as the two broke into hysterical laughter.

ii

Jake Hanssen sat in the big chair directly across from Douglas Vorrals, director of the Federal Bureau of Investigation. Hanssen was obviously nervous.

"I've done all I can, Jake. Pulled everything we've got. You've got no choice but to be placed back into police custody tomorrow."

"But—" Hanssen began.

"No," Vorrals interrupted. "No buts. I got you out the first time, and gave you as much time as I could for you to establish this alleged collaborative link between the Freeman kid and Nesterov. We'll keep working on the case, you can be assured of that, but your injunction expires tomorrow."

"I need it extended, Mr. Vorrals, just another two weeks. We traced Page... ahh... Freeman to this small town in western Tennessee called Sardis, and—"

"Enough!" Vorrals scolded. "I'm not going to tell you again! Turn over your badge and report to the fourth district court tomorrow at ten a.m. Is that clear?"

iii

Siro Scribner scribbled some notes on his pad, in between sentences still sneaking nervous glances at the Prophet, who sat across the table from him.

He was initiating the first segment of what would be a regular section in *The Signs of the Times*, a Q & A piece with the Great Prophet of the Modern Age. Though Jimi T. had introduced the pair before, Siro felt very anxious sitting with this man, especially as he sensed that some sort of tension existed between the two.

"So you're saying, Great Teacher, that the Mayans wrote the *Lib Dône Verü?*"

"No, that is not what I am saying," Tæsír Hoc countered. "The Mayans are the first culture to collect the ancient writings of the Great Prophets of the *Kôles*, most of which predate the Hebrew Scriptures. As you can see, the Mayans also included the words of the Great Prophets Ezekiel, Isaiah, and still others who were edited out of the Jewish Bible by the *Ďishalåk*."

Siro nodded his head as he continued to jot down notes. It would have been much easier to tape the interview, but the Prophet had refused this request. Siro had a million questions and continually had to prioritize them in his head.

"And what language were these writings in? Some of these words look like Latin or maybe Spanish."

The Prophet responded with a smile of approval. "Very good, my brother. Actually, the vast majority of the writings were in the language of the ancients, called *Seph Aṇtíos*. It was the first language of existence, yet was obliterated from the lips of the people by the *Ďishalåk* out of fear, at that tower which you know as Babel."

Siro's eyes lit up. "You mean those at the Tower of Babel were—"

"They were the *Čidentûl* who had learned the truth. Still, their small community and limited connection proved to be no match for the destructive force of the *Ďishalåk*."

Siro wrote a few more notes then looked up from his pad. "You know, I don't remember all of this being written in the Book."

The Prophet nodded in acknowledgment. "Most of what I speak to you of is in the Book, yet piecemeal, scattered throughout different texts. I am completing the final section of the Book, the Testament of Hoc, which will neatly clarify all the questions which the masses may have."

"And from what source will you write this testament?"

The Tæsír eyed Siro intently, then released what appeared to be a smirk on his face. "You forget, my brother, that I have nearly full access to the *Kôles*. In meditation, I can draw from the collective wisdom of the ages. Not all at once, mind you, for that is impossible in our incarnate form. This is why each testament is nothing more than a portion of the greater truth, pieces of a jigsaw puzzle, if you will. I am here to provide the final piece, so as to give the entire world the full likeness of our purpose."

14

"A great sect arose which, taking for its motto the good and happiness of man, worked in the darkness of conspiracy to make the happiness of humanity a prey for itself."

– The Duke of Brunswick

i

"I really do not like stealing cars from little old ladies, Nathan."

Simon was really only mildly annoyed, being fully aware of what few alternatives there actually were. The woman had left the car running while she stepped into the store, and neither Nathan nor Simon hesitated to jump at the opportunity. Simon was able to temporarily deactivate the *i-Nav* system, but it would automatically re-engage—and lock on—within twenty-four hours. He would have to employ some serious rewiring before that time to cover their trail.

Nathan shrugged. "I really don't know what else we could've done. But we've got some new problems to deal with now."

Simon looked over towards him. "What do you mean?"

Nathan looked back at his friend, and against his better judgment, responded truthfully. "That man that tried to shoot us, he is with the Russian Syndicate, you know, the mafia. I guess he thought I was dead too, but now that he knows I'm alive, he'll be coming after me with everything he's got, that's for sure."

Simon was in utter shock. "What? Why would the Mafia want anything to do with you? I don't understand, is *that* who was after you when you came to my house?"

Nathan shook his head. "No, that was the FBI. They just—"

"The FBI? What did y—?"

"They want to pull me back into their Witness Protection Program, which ain't worth shit, and I don't trust them. I think I've somehow outstayed my welcome."

Simon was so inundated with racing thoughts that he could not think of where to begin with questions. Yet, he still made a vain attempt to gain more insight.

"Nathan, I… how did… what did you…"

Nathan took a deep breath, then held up his hand to indicate that Simon did not have to prod further. "I can probably clear a lot of this up for you real easy, Simon. I guess you're the only friend in the world I've got left, and if I can't trust you, I'm damned anyway."

Simon nodded in acknowledgment of Nathan's statement and apprehensively awaited whatever revelations his friend was about to provide him.

"My name… my name isn't really Nathan Page. It's Nathaniel Freeman."

Simon continued to stare blankly at Nathan, with an occasional glance back at the road. Nathan looked back at him and watched as an expression of realization slowly crept across Simon's face.

"Oh God…"

Nathan broke his gaze from Simon and sat back in his seat, taking in the midnight scenery, as his friend wrestled with his own thoughts and conclusions.

The two drove in silence for another two hours, and finally Nathan spoke up. "I've got to be honest, Simon. I haven't got a clue as to what to do from here, or where to go."

Simon maintained his steady gaze forward as he drove. "I-I think I may have an idea."

"Shoot."

"Well," Simon began. "I heard that Joey Escario is now playing in some band out in LA. You know, the nightclub scene."

Nathan looked curiously at Simon. "Little Joey, huh? How's he doing?"

"Better I guess," Simon answered. "He was real messed up after the… the incident. Spent a few months in a state psychiatric facility. He came out and was able to convince a judge to emancipate him. Guess the state was just itching to give up custody of him anyway."

"Frikkin'-A."

"Yeah, and only a few months ago, I got a clipping sent to me in the mail—I guess from Joey. He's in a band called *Benedictus*."

Nathan thought for a moment and became aware of the cautious glances that Simon was making in his direction. It was clear he was still trying to reconcile Nathan's true identity with the friend he had shared memories with over the past six years.

I'll need to regain his trust.

Finally, Nathan spoke.

"Why not? We've got nowhere else to turn."

Simon nodded his head, and Nathan spoke up again. "I'm going to catch some z's if you don't mind."

"Not at all," Simon responded as he watched Nathan climb into the back seat. A moment later, while squirming to get comfortable, Nathan spoke to him from the back of the vehicle.

"Well, what do you know?"

Simon looked in the rear-view mirror, a curious expression on his face. "What?"

Nathan leaned up towards the front seat, holding something in his hand.

"Looks like this little old lady was having some second thoughts about her precious God."

Simon looked down and grinned as he saw a copy of the *Book of Given Truths* resting in Nathan's hands.

ii

"Jake! Jake, wait up!"

Jake Hanssen considered ignoring the voice that called out from behind him. He was about to leave the Federal Bureau of Investigation building for perhaps the last time when he stopped to see Anton Lefebvre running his way. Hanssen wore an expression of defeat on his face. His thoughts circled around the idea of a life inside a cell surrounded by hundreds of men who would just love to get their hands on a law-enforcement officer "gone bad."

"What is it, Anton?" he asked disinterestedly.

"We just got news over the wire. Nesterov's daughter, Vanya Ciotola, is dead. What's more is they ran a make on a car they pulled out of a nearby lake, and it turns out it's the one the Freeman kid was driving."

Hanssen was staring at Lefebvre wide eyed. "Son of a b——"

"Yeah, the car had a good number of bullet holes in it, but they lifted some fingerprints of both the Freeman kid *and* some of Nesterov's boys off of it."

Hanssen's look of interest transformed into one of exuberance. "That confirms it. That confirms it for me!"

"There's more. We also lifted some of the Freeman kid's fingerprints from inside Vanya Ciotola's house. He's the prime suspect in her murder now."

Hanssen looked confused. "Wait, I don't get it." He turned away, running both hands through his thinning hair. "It makes no damn sense."

"Tell me about it," Lefebvre agreed. "One last thing, Jake. An old lady had her car ripped off not three kilometers from the scene of the crime, and within two hours of when they estimate that Vanya Ciotola was murdered. A clerk gave a description that matched the Freeman kid and his friend, Wilson. Said they headed south."

Hanssen tried to pull together all the facts in his head but was unable to do so. A new thought emerged.

"Nesterov was to be brought in for questioning yesterday for that murder in Ephesus. Did he get formally charged? Is he in custody?"

Lefebvre shook his head. "No. He came in with his hotshot lawyer. There wasn't enough to detain him at the time. But the locals still feel that they're going to be able to get an indictment any day."

Hanssen thought for a moment, straining to grasp the common thread in all this information. He could not, but one thing seemed to be apparent. Freeman had killed Vanya Ciotola, probably out of revenge for the death of his parents, and now Nesterov was going to kill him, in a manner that was sure to leave egg on the face of the Bureau once again.

"That stupid little prick," Hanssen murmured to himself.

But he had something else to worry about now. The evidence now seemed to point *against* a collaborative relationship between Nesterov and Harold Freeman… unless the kid never knew of the alliance. In this scenario, Hanssen's options were growing weaker and weaker, but his vendetta was not.

He looked to Lefebvre. "Anton, I'm required to turn myself in in less than an hour to the federal authorities. But if I do that, I'll lose whatever chance I have to clear my name. I'll spend the rest of my life in prison. We've got one, and perhaps two fugitives from the law now. It's my only chance. I've got to at least go down swinging."

Lefebvre looked back steadily at Hanssen. "What are you asking me for, Jake?"

Hanssen responded carefully. "A dozen men who aren't too chicken-ass to stand up for what's right no matter what that corrupt bastard Vorrals says."

Lefebvre smiled. "Give me an hour."

iii

It was several minutes after three in the afternoon when Annie D. heard the knock at the door. She had just completed praying her chaplet, experiencing a general sense of peace.

Jesus, I trust in You, she mused one last time as she ambled towards the door.

She opened it and there stood Father Daniel Ananias. One look in his eyes made it instantly clear that something was wrong, dreadfully wrong.

Before the priest was even able to get a word out, something at the core of Annie's being revealed the difficult truth to her.

TRYST

"Dear Jesus," she breathed as she felt her knees begin to give way.

Father Daniel caught Annie D. as she crumbled downward, calling out the name of her last child. In truth, she wept for all of her children and refused to be comforted because they were no more...

15

The *Ďishalăk* had existed, in some form since the inception of the Physical Entity, ordaining themselves as protectors of its tangible existence. These two beings, though appearing to be full life forms, existed outside of the *Kŏles*, and had no connection, growth, or lifecycle as would be part of being within the realm of the Spiritual Entity.

The *Ďishalăk* grew resentful and jealous of the *Kŏles*, and viewed Her as a threat to their temporal power. And indeed She was! By assimilating the essence of the Physical Entity, the *Kŏles* had inadvertently accelerated the process of tangible disintegration. Still, She was the only hope of perpetuating the existence of the essence of the Physical Entity.

Leviat N: 15-20
Book of Given Truths

i

Nathan found himself floating in darkness again. There was a brief moment of terror when he feared he had returned to the endless abyss of himself. But then, out of the nothingness, came a spark of light.

The light grew in its brilliance, and Nathan felt himself being propelled towards it. As he reached the luminous source, he came to realize that it was a doorway within some mystical lighthouse. He hesitated out of fear when a moment later a figure emerged from the entrance.

TRYST

The being stood perhaps slightly above average height. Its hair was jet-black, and its eyes glowed crimson red. It appeared to be masculine and wore a crystal pendant on a neck chain which bore the symbol Nathan now recognized as the Seal. A black cape hung down from the figure's shoulders, which matched the dark boots and gloves. A ring on his left hand glowed the same crimson color as its eyes.

"Come to me," the figure called out with a touch of a not clearly discernable accent, *"and I will protect you."*

A familiar voice cried out from behind Nathan, and then…

He awoke with a start. Nathan jerked his head to the right, then left. Slowly, consciousness returned to him, and he realized that he was in the back seat of the car. Simon glanced in the rear-view mirror.

"What's going on back there, Nathan?" he asked.

Nathan shook his head and sat up. "I-I guess I'm dreaming a bit heavy." He leaned forward into the front seat, rubbing the sleep from his eyes. "Hey, why don't you take a break and let me drive for a while."

Simon smiled and shook his head. "I told you, not a chance. I know your driving record just a bit too well."

Nathan provided a slight trace of a smile then sat back. Simon was engaging in a great deal more zigzagging through differing directions in his navigation, not fully confident the rewiring on the *i-Nav* system was effective. The result was many detours through back roads and small towns. Nathan looked out the window and his eye was caught by a billboard they were approaching.

It had a picture of a man who looked like cleaner-cut version of Charlton Heston's Moses on it, with a large image of the now familiar marking called the Seal. The words read, "The Way of Mystic Realism." Underneath the headshot, the man was identified as "Tæsír Hoc, Prophet of the Modern Age."

Nathan looked down at the copy of the *Book of Given Truths* on the floor and picked it up. He had been feeling less and less inclined to provide excuses for his intrigue in the book. He opened it and again began to read.

About an hour later, Nathan looked up from the book, and spoke.

"You know, Simon, there's some pretty wild stuff in this book."

Simon looked briefly in the rear-view mirror as Nathan continued.

"It claims the original texts were maintained by the Mayans, and that they eventually had to flee their homeland because of opposition to it. It even says that a small sect of Mayans immigrated all the way to Kashmir, where they integrated with Trappist monks, and further expanded their teachings of this Mystic Realism."

"So where are these Mayans supposed to be now?" Simon inquired.

"Well, it claims that the Trappist monks, those horny bastards, bred with the Mayan refugees. Eventually they were expelled from the order, and the entire bunch fled the country to some island in the Pacific."

"Sounds a bit farfetched for me."

Nathan shrugged, "Yeah, I guess so. Still, if nothing else, it's a pretty cool story. In the foreword section, it says this dude Tæsír Hoc was born on that island and is the first of this group to go public into the civilized world. It says he's the last of the Great Teachers, and will be completing the final testament of this book."

Simon tilted his head inquisitively. "What do you mean when you say he's the first to go public?"

"I guess that many other individuals over time have left the island to help out mankind in one way or another... you know, keep us from getting too far off track. But for the most part, their responsibility was to protect the ancient writings and prepare for the coming of what they call the Modern Age, which will signal the time of the Messiah."

Simon suddenly slowed the car, and Nathan looked up to see what was going on. A mass of hundreds of people lined both sides of the highway carrying signs and chanting. One sign read *"Beware: The Antichrist is among us"* another *"Prepare ye for the return of the Lord!"* Many wore T-shirts with a slashed out picture of Tæsír Hoc on it, dubbing him "The False Prophet."

"Would you look at that," Simon exclaimed, with more than a hint of concern in his voice. He pulled the car to a halt as he and Nathan looked on.

The crowd parted on the right side, and Nathan was able to spot several individuals being led through the horde. He opened his mouth in incredulity as he saw three male youths, two black and one Hispanic, stripped completely naked, being led through the crowd. Their hands were bound behind their backs, and their chests bled from where Nathan could see that a rough version of the Seal had been carved into them.

TRYST

"Oh my God!" Simon gasped.

He brought the vehicle to a full stop as the youths were led out into the middle of the street and made to get on their knees. Simon looked to Nathan. "What do I do?"

Nathan couldn't respond, watching in bewilderment as he realized that the expressions on the boys' faces were not of terror, but instead, serenity.

Three individuals in hooded white sheets emerged from the crowd, and stood behind each youth. The crowd cheered and chanted as a fourth figure stepped out of the throng. His sheet did not cover his face. The crowd's shouting slowly died down.

"BEHOLD!" he called out. "BEHOLD THE CHILDREN OF SATAN! LET THE SPILLING OF THEIR BLOOD BE A MESSAGE TO ALL WHO FOLLOW THE BEAST!"

A cheer rang through the horde as each of the hooded figures pulled a semiautomatic weapon from underneath their robes, pointing them directly at the youths.

"Oh sh—"

Just then, a rumbling sound began to overtake the clamor of the crowd. Simon looked to Nathan, utterly terrified, paralyzed as what to do. They looked back and watched on helplessly as the ground began to shake. The unhooded man called out.

"DO NOT FEAR, MY CHILDREN. THE PATH OF THE LORD IS—"

A bolt of lightning shot out of the now darkened sky, striking the preacher where he stood. His charred body fell limply to the ground. The horde began screaming, dispersing frantically in every direction. Nathan scrambled into the front seat, and he caught a glimpse of the youths still kneeling in the middle of the street amidst the chaos. They had not attempted to move and maintained their expressions of serenity on their faces. Their lips seemed to be moving in synchronicity.

"DRIVE SIMON! DRIVE!"

Simon hit the accelerator and swerved to avoid the young men, who continued to kneel without taking notice of the cataclysm taking place around them. Nathan watched, petrified, as cracks in the Earth's surface began to open up, spewing out reddish gas and enveloping most of the now-terror-stricken mob. Though Simon attempted to avoid the people scrambling across the street, he was not completely successful and struck someone.

The body flew up onto the hood of the car, and the man's head cracked against the windshield. Both Simon and Nathan screamed simultaneously. Nathan watched in terror as the eyes in the now misshapen head met his.

"He comes for you, Nathan. He comes for you…"

ii

Alexandre stepped away from the gravesite of his last child. He had Vanya laid to rest next to her sister, brother, and two nephews, as he felt she would have wanted. He felt utterly numb. Annie D. stood on the opposite side of the grave wearing dark glasses and a veil, as still as an icon.

"Annie, I—"

"Get away from me," she breathed smoothly, yet dripping with fathomless venom.

Nesterov looked down, turned awkwardly, and began to walk away.

Annie D. tried not to look up to witness the two-dozen law enforcement officers that stood along the police line of the still designated crime scene. It was fitting, in a disgusting sort of way. She looked at the midsized tree—one that had given her a curious sense of consolation in the past—now serving as a posting point for the police tape to wrap around. It should have been covered with buds of the mid-spring, but it was not. If the gentle melody she had once heard in her spirit was again attempting to resonate, she could not, would not, hear it.

Felix Amosov moved rapidly to catch up to his boss, whose pace still quickened. Soon Amosov was in stride with Nesterov, who did not look up at him.

"Alex," Amosov began. "Alex, the guys are waiting for the word. They want to put every man on tracking this Freeman kid down and making him suffer—suffer badly. Just give me the word, Alex, and we will hunt him, we will hurt him, and then we will kill him as many times as we can."

TRYST

Nesterov looked at Amosov almost blankly. "This Freeman family... this Freeman family has caused me more pain than anyone could possibly imagine. They... they have taken my entire family from me. I have no one left. Do you understand, Felix? No one!"

Amosov strained not to look back at Annie D., then nodded in acknowledgment. "Yes, Alex, we realize that. Just give us the word, and he is history."

Nesterov stopped where he stood and looked aimlessly forward. Slowly, he nodded his head. "Yes, yes, you have the word. But I want to be there, I want to watch the little *ebanatyi pidaraz* die!"

iii

"Well, isn't this a surprise? Liz Lewton, the whore of the Modern Age!"

"Delilah?"

The incensed Delilah Hagarot had not expected to find her old gossip-mate at the terminal point of her quest. Yet she was determined to get answers to the question which had haunted her these past three years.

"Yes. Surprised, are you, Liz? So, are you his new little mistress now? I would think he'd be looking for someone much... *younger.*"

Liz was momentarily speechless, but it did not take more than a moment for her surprise to transform into her own form of ire.

"Listen, *Del,*" she breathed. "I have no idea what you are talking about. If you have a problem with the Prophet—"

"Ohh, the Prophet?" Delilah retorted in a tone dripping with sarcasm. "Is that what he's calling himself now? How rich!" She leaned across the receptionist desk, close enough to force Liz to lean back slightly. "Now you listen to me, Liz. You tell old *Sammy* that I came by, and that I want answers. I know he knows where my son is, and unless he wants his sordid past all over the newswire, I suggest he find some break in his busy schedule to see me."

Liz could not prevent a devilish smirk from creeping across her face. "*Sordid,* Del? Ohh, that's impressive. I didn't know your vocabulary ever made it out of the third grade."

Delilah's eyes widened as her face flushed. She started to lean back, then suddenly jerked forward, spitting on Liz's face. Liz quickly started grasping for a tissue to wipe the spittle from her. Delilah stepped back and fully stood up, satisfied with herself, and eyed the rest of the meticulously ornamented front office.

"You've done real well for yourself, Liz, haven't you?" Delilah continued to nod, maintaining her smug expression. "But you have no idea what you're dealing with. You let good ol' Sammy know that I'll be back."

With that, Delilah turned and began her dramatic exit, though it was tempered by the words that Liz called out from behind her.

"I don't know that I'd want to put myself in the position of being a liability to him…"

16

Allied Press ~

CHICAGO - In a growing pattern that has left many voicing concern, the *Chicago Times* announced its merger with the rapidly growing news media conglomerate *The Signs of the Times*.

"This is not a merger," stated one senior employee who asked to remain anonymous. "This is nothing short of a hostile takeover. Today, a great newspaper was absorbed by the new 'Big Brother'."

The recent takeover is the fifth in what appears to be a growing pattern of expansionism. To date, *Times* Magazine, the *New York Inquirer*, the *Wall Street Chronicle*, the *Los Angeles Globe*, and the *Washington Sun* have all been absorbed by the media conglomerate.

Siro Scribner, senior editor-in-chief of *The Signs of the Times*, described the merger as "a cooperative effort in reporting the unbiased truth."

i

Simon looked over at Nathan, who was still sleeping. Nathan twitched, tossed and turned. He had refused to tell to Simon what the dreams were about, but Simon knew they were slowly but surely pushing his friend to the edge.

Nathan might have had a bad dream or two at the beginning of their trip, but ever since that mob scene two weeks before, Simon would guess they haunted him every time he closed his eyes. He himself had not yet shaken the unnerving sensation that still emanated from within him, and he found his mind questioning as to whether they had actually witnessed the scene.

He had continued to drive a random zigzag pattern across the country, at this point using exclusively back roads and trying to avoid traveling in any type of pattern that the feds, or the Mafia, might trace. He had given one last shot at fully deactivating the *i-Nav* system the night before, but he still carried a great concern over being tracked. Perhaps a single vehicle with no signal was as easy to discover as one with a signal.

Utterly bored and wanting to get his mind off the worry, Simon turned on the radio, searching for a news station. On his way to finding one, he flipped through at least three stations playing Jimi T. Expo, cursing his artificial hand as it struck the wrong buttons. Finally, he reached a station with a news voice:

> *"...violence in Eurabia has reached a crescendo, as the oil-revenue-dependent nations of the Islamic Union seek to contain the Non-Muslim minorities..."*

He hit the seek button a couple more times, then stopped.

> *"...in a growing trend of religious violence, Hispanic Christians and New York Jews clashed today in the suburb of..."*

"You've got to be kidding me." He hit the seek button again.

> *"...President Lang's veto was overridden, allowing for further restrictions to be placed on religious institutions..."*

Seek button.

TRYST

"...at this rate, with the surging U.S. economy, the once massive national debt will be paid off within three years..."

"One more chance, radio, and then that's it!" He hit the seek button a final time.

"In an announcement broadcast by The Signs of the Times satellite radio network, Jimi T. Expo has selected his third band member, keyboardist Bobby Gandolph. Gandolph was the founding member of the group Night Rapture and is viewed by many to be the premier..."

Simon flipped the switch off, trying to restrain himself from screaming at the top of his lungs. He took several deep breaths, but could not get himself to relax. "You're losing it, Simon," he said aloud. "The entire world is going to hell in a hand basket, and you're gonna lose your damned mind!"

ii

Nathan was back. He knew it immediately. He was back in that plane of existence which seemed to transcend dreams, drawing all of his internal miseries into one, horrible reality.

He looked out across the desert, where he could see a cloud of sand being kicked up. Something was moving towards him at a rapid pace. In another moment, he was able to discern a horse carrying a dark rider. The rider's approach was swift, and he pulled the horse to a stop perhaps five meters from Nathan. He was dressed all in black and looked like someone out of colonial times—save his eyes, which glowed crimson red.

The rider beckoned to Nathan, and Nathan took a step forward to oblige when he stopped dead in his tracks. Tied up and being dragged behind the steed were two men whom Nathan immediately recognized as Jake Hanssen and Alexandre Nesterov. They had the Seal branded into their foreheads.

"Come to me, Nathan," the rider called out, *"and they will never harm you or those you care for ever again."*

Nathan was about to speak when he heard a child weeping from behind him. He turned and saw the back of a man filling in a grave atop a large mound with a shovel. To the man's right, a body hung from a noose attached to an old oak tree. Its head was covered with a sack, but Nathan found something vaguely familiar about the *Judas Priest* shirt the corpse wore.

He heard the crying again and realized it was coming from somewhere atop the mound. Nathan walked up towards the gravesite and watched as the gravedigger continued to go about his work, paying Nathan no mind. Nathan came within three meters of the grave and stared curiously at the gravestone, which read "The Bastard Twin".

A voice cried out, and Nathan jerked his head downwards to see a little child of no more than six years of age crying up at him.

"Don't listen to him, Nate... He lies!"

Another mound of dirt from the gravedigger's shovel was thrown onto the boy's head, and he began spitting the dirt from his mouth.

"Hey you, stop that!" Nathan called out to the gravedigger, but he did not respond and continued to shovel soil upon the boy.

"I SAID STOP IT!"

Nathan reached up, grabbed the man's shoulder and wheeled him around.

What Nathan saw, smiling back at him with a menacing grin, was none other than his own image.

iii

"What do you mean we still can't find him?"

Douglas Vorrals was furious, but what many of his men did not realize was that he was also scared. He had known Jake Hanssen to occasionally cause problems, but none like this.

It had now been more than two weeks since Hanssen had missed his court date, and he was now designated as a federal fugitive. Vorrals told the Federal Court judge that he would personally see to it that Hanssen was brought into custody. But now all leads were gone, disappearing along with a dozen or so of the Bureau's men.

TRYST

Unbeknownst to the rest of his men, what frightened Vorrals the most, however, was the unmarked envelope which he had found on his desk the morning following Hanssen's disappearance. To the best of his knowledge, no one else was aware of its contents, and Vorrals intended to keep it that way.

The note read simply:

Dougie,

On my way to tie up some unfinished business. I suggest you don't try to bring me in, unless you want me to testify to the fact that you gave the order to waste the Freeman kid.

Have a nice day...

Jake

Vorrals was not about to bow to the threats of a wanted fugitive. Nor was he about to let that fugitive live to carry out his threat.

He looked up to his men. "I want everyone we've got on this, and I'm coming along to personally see this one out."

17

"The great majority of people have a strong need for authority which they can admire, to which they can submit, and which dominates and sometimes even ill-treats them. It is the longing for the father that lives in each of us from his childhood days, for the same father whom the hero of legend boasts of having overcome."

– Sigmund Freud

i

"How much farther to the nightclub?" Nathan asked.

Simon squinted his eyes, trying to see clearly through all the bright Los Angeles neon signs that reflected off his wire-rimmed glasses. It was a few minutes before midnight, and the city was bustling with activity. Though the artificial lighting made the scene even brighter than daylight, it could never sufficiently mask the encompassing darkness.

"If that dude was right, it should be another six blocks up on the left."

Nathan gazed on intently, watching each person as they drove by.

"What's eating you?" Simon inquired.

Nathan shook his head. "I don't know. I guess coming to see Joey here kind of brings back the whole thing. I still have a lot of questions about that night."

Simon replied monotone, not diverting his eyes from the road. "Don't we all…"

Nathan looked back to his friend, trying to decide whether or not this was the time to ask.

He swallowed and cautiously proceeded. "Simon?"

"Yeah, what?"

"Do you remember what was going on… you know… right before it happened?"

Simon looked over at him, and Nathan could see he was treading on very delicate ground.

"I've tried to forget."

Nathan looked up to the street and pointed. "There it is, the Spitting Cobra Lounge."

Simon slowed the vehicle and pulled into the parking lot of the club, finding a parking space relatively easily. The sign read "Live Music – *BENEDICTUS* – All Original Compositions – tonight."

Simon put the car into park and turned off the ignition. Nathan, never one to let go of a thought, began again.

"I remember Jon moving back towards the microphone—"

"Why you gotta do this, dude?" Simon snapped. "What are you trying to accomplish? And why now? We've been traveling together for nearly two months, and I still don't feel like I know what's going on. Nathan, I mean, I don't know how to even talk to you…" Simon momentarily broke off with a curse, then feeling that a momentum had been sufficiently built up, he continued. "I feel like I don't even know who you are anymore. Like you're not the same person I once knew."

They both sat there for a moment, staring at each other. It was Simon who broke the awkward silence.

"Is there something more to all of this than you're telling me?"

Nathan looked down. "No, Simon, no there's… well, yes… I suppose in a way."

Nathan knew he was being incoherent, but he himself was unable to sort through all of the thoughts, the lies, and the outright bizarre images in his head. How could he begin to communicate to another what he did not understand himself? Had he been holding back from Simon? Had he put a wedge between himself and the only living friend he had?

"I am sorry, Simon. You're right. There is more to all of this, but I can't begin to understand what that 'more' is, and if you want to leave right now, just drop me off and head on out. No hard feelings."

They sat, staring at each other. Nathan could see the moisture begin to well up in Simon's eyes. "I don't have any place else to go, Nathan," he whispered solemnly as his eyes slowly fell to his artificial hand. "I don't have any purpose left in my life."

"It's just that, that night—"

"That night? That mother—" Simon's sadness quickly escalated to rage as he released a series of expletives. "Give it up, Nathan! It's ancient history! It's—"

"But I've got to know!" Nathan shot back.

"Know what?"

Nathan took a deep breath, taking just a moment to let the tension subside. "When Jon was just a step away from the microphone... before anything happened... Joey screamed out for him to stop. *Nothing* had happened yet, except for Jon being out in la-la land. Joey saw something, or *knew* something was up. And I want to know what it was."

Nathan met Simon's eyes and what he saw was no longer anger but fear. "Nathan, do we have to—?"

"I've got to do this."

Simon watched as Nathan got out of the car and headed for the entrance. He hesitated for a moment and took a deep breath himself before getting out of the vehicle.

When Simon and Nathan entered the nightclub, the band, *Benedictus*, was finishing off its final set. The pair was able to find a seat relatively easily, as the band apparently did not draw a large audience.

Nathan looked up to see none other than Joey Escario himself banging away relentlessly at the drums. Nathan allowed the preceding intensity to dissipate and smiled to himself. Joey had probably put on about twenty kilograms—none of it good—and likely had not cut his hair since their last meeting. What saddened Nathan, however, was that it was obvious that Joey was strung out on some type of drug.

Nathan ordered a beer, while Simon ordered his signature tonic water, and the two sat back as the lead vocalist ripped into his final verse:

> *I feel a peace that tears my heart and soul*
> *The mountains quake as I fight to lose control*

TRYST

A sea of pain serves to keep my mind in hold
The road is wide, but the bridge is all I know

Simon and Nathan exchanged glances as Nathan started to get up.

"No, Nathan, don't do it!"

Nathan turned and leaned forward, bringing his face up within centimeters of Simon's. "That's *Personal Demon* they're singing, Jon's composition! Joey sold him out... the son of a bitch sold him out!"

Nathan turned, pushed through the tables, and went straight for Joey. Joey had only a moment to look up and see what was coming at him.

"Oh sh—"

Nathan crashed through the drum set, plowing Joey over and pinning him to the floor. "You son of a bitch! You sold him out! You son of a bitch!"

Joey looked up at the madman who had tackled him and recognition spread across his face. "Oh Nathan... oh God! I thought—"

"Give it up, Escario! You knew what was going to happen to him, didn't you?"

Joey burst into tears as he struggled. "No, no! I didn't know they were going to kill him. I swear to God. I didn't know!"

Nathan felt hot tears filling his own eyes as he repeatedly slammed Joey's head into the floor. "Why, Joey, why did you do it? He was your friend! Was it for money you mother—?" Nathan continued to pound away at Joey, both verbally and physically.

Joey was beyond hysterical. "I had no choice! They gave me no choice!"

Nathan slowed himself for a moment, trying to digest what Joey had just said.

They?

Before any subsequent words could reach his lips, two large hands grabbed Nathan by the shoulders, wheeled him around, and he had no sooner focused his eyes when his lights went out.

ii

"I think we've got him, Jake!"

Jake Hanssen turned around to look at Anton Lefebvre, who had just excitedly hung up the phone.

"Nathan Freeman spent last night in an LA county jail after a bar fight."

Hanssen jumped up. "Do they still have him in custody?"

Lefebvre shook his head. "No. Simon Wilson bailed him out this morning. But we have the name of the motel they're staying at."

"Did this information get to Bureau headquarters?"

"Yeah, that's how I got it. But one of our guys intercepted it before it got out."

Hanssen smiled. "Excellent. Book all of our guys on the next flight out to LA."

iii

Alexandre Nesterov sat on the back porch of his cottage gazing out aimlessly across the Lake of the Ozarks. The water was still, yet not stagnant. It reflected what Alexandre desired for his soul.

How Annie would love this view.

Cold Springs, Missouri was definitely all he could have ever wanted in a retirement spot, save the fact that he was alone—alone in a way that seemed to permeate his spirit with a slow, suffocating *absence*. Each day he would wake up, wishing he had not, then come out to this same spot to sit and start in on his bottle of Wild Turkey for the day.

Felix Amosov had settled into the cottage next to him. He seemed to have his own demons to battle, shunning the nicotine gum for his newfound vice of Honduran cigars; a perfect companion for his imported Vodka from the motherland. He had loved little, and now he suffered little.

"Alex."

So numb was his interior that Alexandre did not even jump at the sudden approach of his neighbor.

"So what is so important that you must disturb my grief, Felix?" he inquired listlessly.

Felix, cigar in mouth with an odor that preceded him, stepped up and opened the porch door. Alexandre did not look up as his friend took a seat across from him. "Well, Alex, I am not sure that you were aware of this, but I asked Andrey to keep an eye on that character Hanssen from the Bureau."

Alexandre frowned. "For what purpose?"

"No purpose, Alex. Does there always need to be a purpose? Andrey needs to be kept busy so as to keep him from beating up on all of his daughter's boyfriends."

Alexandre could not help but provide a trace of a lethargic smile.

"Would you like a cigar, Alex? I have three more cases at the house."

Alexandre looked back over to Felix, some life finally starting to show in his face. "I would sooner request a bullet in my head, Felix. So why are you still tailing this pathetic little man? He is of no consequence to us."

"Well, he has apparently gone on some Lone Ranger crusade and skipped bond."

Alexandre provided an affirming nod. "Good for him. Life is too short to live it out rotting in a cell." He thought a moment longer, then looked at his comrade more intently. "So what does this have to do with me, Felix? Has the *bliad'* decided to come after me? At this point, I may very well welcome him into my home."

"Ahh, no, Alex, he is not coming after you. He is going after the kid."

This was an interesting development.

"Freeman?"

"That is right. I get the impression he is losing his marbles, as they say. Anyway, we have just listened in on one of his phone calls, and he has tracked the kid down in Los Angeles."

"Does he have him?" Alexandre asked, suddenly feeling further signs of life moving within his spirit.

"No, Alex, he is flying out of Norfolk International Airport in less than an hour. If we pull some strings and get a chartered jet out from here, we should have at least an hour jump on him."

Alexandre hesitated. Only three weeks earlier he had given the order to have this boy brought in so that he could be made to suffer before the man his family had so foolishly plagued. But with each day passing, and each phone call Annie D. ignored, a part of Alexandre would die a little more inside. Curiously, along with this apparent interior decay of self, his previously insatiable desire for revenge seemed to be waning. Was this a good thing? Could it be possible that for the first time in his life, Alexandre Nesterov would give a man a pass?

In a certain sense, Alexandre himself was free and clear. The authorities, with a little financial encouragement, had decided not to pursue the case against him in the death of Jeffrey Chardin. All other charges against him over the years had one by one fallen away, as if he were untouchable. Could he really just let it go?

Felix looked at his comrade intently, not knowing how to read his hesitance. A thought struck him, which he then posed to his boss. "You know, Alex, you do not even need to be a part of this one. Let me and the boys finish this one off. The kid is not worth your time. I will just let you know it is done."

What would Annie think? Would she take me back if she believed I had changed?

But he was seventy years old. Perhaps too many years to seek new stripes. He wrestled with the thought.

Could I really change?

"Alex?"

Could Annie ever forgive me?

"Alex?"

Would she even permit herself to hear the sound of my voice?

Felix, slightly flustered at this point, crushed out the last bit of his stogie and stood. "That settles it then, Alex. I will handle this one myself. I will return in a few days with good news."

18

"To forgive is to set a prisoner free
and discover that prisoner was you."

– Lewis B. Smedes

i

Simon continued to place calls on the motel's phone, trying to track down Joey. Nathan sat up on the other bed, holding an ice pack over his left eye with one hand and holding the *Book of Given Truths* open with the other.

"You know, Simon," he started without looking up from the book, "according to this, all the problems that have occurred in the history of the world are the doing of only two semi-immortal men."

Simon looked at Nathan, still somewhat angry. "Yeah, and I'm looking at one of them right now."

Nathan put the book down. "Look, Simon, I screwed up. I know that. But I did find some of the information I was looking for, I—"

"There are other ways to get— *Hello?*"

Nathan stood up and moved towards the sink to change out his ice pack. He listened as Simon spoke on the phone.

"Yes, I'm a friend of Joseph Escario, and I've been trying to locate him for the past two days... yes we... we used to be in a band together... he... he WHAT? When?"

Nathan turned towards Simon, who was now looking back towards him helplessly. "Which hospital is he in? What? He got transferred to a... do... do you have the address?"

Nathan moved over to the bed and sat as Simon reached for a pad and pen, scribbling out the address being recited to him over the phone.

"Thanks, thank you very much. Bye." Simon slowly hung up the phone.

"What's going on?"

Simon looked at Nathan, staring in disbelief. "It's Joey, he OD'd about an hour after we left the bar. He got transferred to a psychiatric facility today. They say he's really fried."

"Oh shit," Nathan breathed as he buried his head in his hands. "What have I done?"

Simon looked at Nathan briefly, then stood up. "Dude, we've got to go see him—now!"

Nathan looked up at Simon weakly. Simon moved towards him, placing his good hand on Nathan's shoulder. "Listen, dude, don't go schizo now. It's not going to take your friends long to realize it was a bogus motel address we gave to the police. We've got to get out of town. But first, you got to square things with Joey."

Nathan slowly nodded his head and got up from the bed.

ii

Annie D. Nesterov reached for the phone once again, then once again, pulling her hand back each time. The level of rage she had attained over the call the day before was unprecedented. After slamming down the receiver, she had almost immediately picked it back up to apologize—to forgive.

So much had happened. So much that could never be changed. It was only fitting—she thought—that Alexandre would suffer some as a Divine consequence to his own actions. Forgiving him too soon would amount to little more than cheap grace—and would probably provide little incentive to leave his sinful ways behind him once and for all, would it not?

Her mind raced with scripture verses and voices of faithful acquaintances who screamed to the contrary of her line of thinking. Yet within her, Annie D. experienced a hardness of heart not before known in her lifetime. Surely she would need to confess this. Surely, one day she would need to forgive.

Aye, Lord. But not today. And then with sad resolution she mused, *Forgive me, Lord. I've not the strength today…*

iii

"This kid is screwing with us, and I don't like it one bit!" Hanssen vented to Anton Lefebvre in their hotel room.

"Listen, Jake, he's still in the city. I'm sure of it. We'll find him, one way or another, we'll find him."

Hanssen plopped down on the bed. "This whole damn thing's been a nightmare. How can they let the primary suspect in a murder walk out of an L.A. jail?"

Lefebvre looked at his partner steadily. "Come on, Jake, you know California didn't take too kindly to the national isolationist policies. They've been pretty anti-fed throughout. We shouldn't expect any help from them."

Unable to sit still, Hanssen rose from the bed and walked over to the window. He stared intently at the city life below. "I just don't know anymore, Anton. I spent almost six years protecting this kid and his family… with my life. And now nothing makes sense. First it seems as if Nesterov wants to rip him limb from limb, then it seems the kid's in tight with Nesterov's grandson, and then he turns around and whacks his best friend's old lady. I just don't get it."

Lefebvre stared evenly at Hanssen, who obviously had something to get off his chest.

"And now, *I'm* a fugitive from the law, and I'm supposed to spend the rest of my life in prison… for… for trying to do the right thing!"

Lefebvre shook his head and got up from his chair. "It's like I said, Jake, the world's going down the toilet. There's more laws on the books now to protect the scum instead of the righteous." He leaned in close to Hanssen's ear and whispered through his teeth. "You can't rely on the government anymore, Jake. It's every man for himself now, and the world doesn't give a damn who wears a badge and who doesn't. It's for *us* to set things right—no matter what the cost."

Hanssen looked to Lefebvre, nodding mechanically. He was right.

"Get the guys together," Hanssen spouted, recapturing his strength. "We've got a piece of scum to catch."

iv

"It seems that the Anointed has formulated quite a... *unique* plan to manifest the Master's will, has he not?"

Luther nodded in acknowledgement to his fellow *Illumini*, Eumenes, attempting to mask his own slight irritation with the 'Mystic King'. "It is unique, I suppose, but not outside of the Great Seraph's realm by any means. I would say that it is... *fitting*."

The one called Marius spoke. "I would say it is quite brilliant. Yet I am curious, why does the Anointed not report on his activities to this Council himself?"

"He trusts my capacity to relay his activities and wishes to this coterie, as I hope this Council itself trusts that I accurately relay its thoughts to him."

"Of that, there is no question, Luther," Anaxagoras assured.

Luther looked to his fellow *Illumini*. It was clear that the nature of their role in the Master's plan was transforming, though *how* was still a mystery to him.

"Perhaps it would be best to address me with my proper title, Tæsír Hoc."

There seemed to be a moment of discord with the Council of twenty-one, even *amusement*, as Cato interjected, "You are new at this, brother, so your request is understandable. Yet it is important not to over-identify with any current persona. You will no doubt assume others in the days to come."

Luther provided a slight nod of acknowledgement, attempting to appear unfazed by the admittedly mild admonishment. Yet his interior was seething with well-seasoned venom. It was *he* that had set all these events in motion at the bidding of their Master. It was *he* that led this coterie. And in the end, it would be *he* that would accept his rightful place at the left-hand of the Great Seraph. On that day, *all* would have to account for the smallest slight directed towards him. And in this court, the antithesis of mercy, he would relish each drop of suffering dispensed in service to infernal justice.

19

i

Nesterov sat in the back seat of the car, while at his side Felix Amosov watched through the tinted glass with binoculars.

"It would appear they are leaving, Alex—the entire bunch." Then, looking back to his boss, he said, "Alex, I am getting too old for this... *you* are getting too old for this. You should not have come—and I never should have told you. Can we not go to a nice hotel, order some take out, and let the boys fill us in later?"

Nesterov did not respond directly, still trying to quash the last vestiges of conscience within him. His final attempt to reestablish some communication with Annie had failed—badly.

"I may be old, but I still know how to settle a score, Felix."

Amosov nodded silently. He had a bad feeling about this entire thing. What was most disconcerting was the look in Nesterov's eyes the day before when he banged violently on Amosov's cottage door, not more than a half-hour after their previous chat on the porch. Something had changed—something not even the half bottle of Wild Turkey could mitigate. Not only would Nesterov be seeing out the demise of Nathan Freeman himself, but he also ordered Andrey Gavrilenkov to "conclude things" with Mikhail Ostankino.

"Do not misunderstand me," Amosov had pleaded, "I have no love for the man. But we are not even certain it was he that ordered the hit on Yerik."

"Do not question me, Felix. This time, we finish everything."

Nesterov's heart rate quickened as he meditated on all that would take place this day. The last fragments of his anxious conscience transformed into exhilaration.

"Let us stay close behind them, Felix, and make sure the rest of our men are mobilized to move quickly. As soon as Hanssen has the Freeman kid, I want everyone we have got to converge on the scene. Then, wait for my word, and we will finish them all off."

Amosov nodded to the driver and then looked back over to Nesterov. "The Freeman kid too?"

Nesterov shook his head as the driver began to pull them out into the traffic. "I need to do something for him fitting of a cold-blooded murderer and son of a *sooka*."

ii

Douglas Vorrals stood up before the three-dozen men he had handpicked for this assignment. The Bureau's private jet was set to land in Los Angeles in less than an hour. The cabin grew quiet, and Vorrals began his semi-prepared speech.

"I first want to emphasize to all of you the importance of this mission. I am embarrassed to say that we are going after one of our own on this one. Jake Hanssen is a man out of control, attempting to fulfill a personal vendetta. He has also coerced a handful of Bureau agents to help him out on this crusade of his. I can't emphasize enough, for the sake of the Bureau, that this mission be kept in the highest classification of confidentiality. You are not to speak to anyone, ever, about what will be taking place over the next few days. Is that understood?"

The entire group nodded affirmatively.

"Very well. This is going to be an airtight operation, and we can't afford any slip-ups. Your orders, directly from the attorney general, are to shoot Jake Hanssen on sight, as well as any other agents who have chosen to take his side. We must put an end to this embarrassment, gentlemen, and get back to performing the fine work of protecting our great nation."

The group was silent. Each of these handpicked men had been bailed out of some ethical indiscretion by the director at one time or another. All were aware that it was quite unlikely that the attorney general would give such an order, let alone having the president's approbation in doing so. Yet none of them cared. A new era was upon them, requiring a new perspective on just about everything. Change was coming, and Douglas Vorrals knew how to seize the day.

iii

"Is all falling into place, *Hocus*?"

"Yes, Your Lordship."

"And you have informed your precious Council?"

"As you requested, I have."

"Then all the actors are ready to play their parts?"

"Yes."

"Very well, then. Let us pay one last visit to a dear old friend."

"As you wish, Your Lordship."

20

i

Nathan and Simon stepped up to the nurse's station, identified themselves as members of Joey's family, and were led through a locked door and down a long hallway.

"I don't think I can do this," Nathan whispered.

Simon provided him with an uncharacteristically stern look. The two reached the door and cautiously peered through the tempered glass.

Joey lay on the bed in the center of the room, looking up at the ceiling, smiling broadly and humming.

Nathan and Simon looked at each other for a moment, waited for a buzzer which accompanied the lock disengagement, then stepped in. Joey dropped his gaze from the ceiling down to his visitors, maintaining a large grin, and chanting quietly.

"They're coming to take me away, ha ha… They're coming to take me away, ho ho, he he, ha ha…"

"Oh Joey," Nathan breathed.

"Run, Joey, run Joey, run!"

Joey broke into childish giggling. Simon stood immobilized, feeling an incredible compulsion to vomit—his previous resoluteness quickly fading. Nathan stepped forward to where Joey lay and looked down to realize that Joey's wrists and ankles were bound to the bed. Joey looked up at Nathan like a puppy dog, panting.

Nathan reached out his hand, touching Joey's cheek. Joey leaned his head into Nathan's touch, closing his eyes, savoring the caress of a human hand.

"It was me, Nathan," he whispered.

Nathan looked down, somewhat stunned, and leaned closer.

"What do you mean, Joey? What was you?"

Joey's mouth quivered into a tenuous smile, as he opened his eyes, staring longingly at his old friend. "It was me that let them kill Jesse."

Nathan felt the side of his face twinge as he once again heard that name called out. He spoke, "You mean Jonathan, right, Joey? Not Jesse, Jonathan."

Joey cackled out loud in a disgusted fashion, jerking his head away from Nathan's hand. "Don't you know anything, man? There's no stinkin' Jonathan! There never was! He's a stinkin' myth!" Joey's anxiety clearly began to escalate as he began speaking, *pleading*, in between pants. "Jesse… now *there's* a real mother—" he unleashed a series of vile curses. "He's the demon seed. He still lives… in my head… but I had to kill him…"

Joey looked away, cackling again, then went silent and lowering his gaze. He began to cry. "It would have been better… had I never been born…"

Nathan looked back towards Simon for help and found that he had, little by little, cowered back into the far corner of the room. "My God…"

"You've got it all wrong, Nathan," Joey suddenly whispered, a moment of complete coherence showing in his eyes. "You believe me to be the betrayer… but in truth, I'm the friend."

Nathan's eyes narrowed. "What are you saying J—"

"You should listen more closely to Jesse, Nathan. All is not as it should be. But there is one thing he asked me to pass on to you."

Nathan glanced back to the shuddering Simon, who was now looking down, his eyes fixed upon his prosthetic. Nathan turned his head back towards Joey as a completely different, somewhat ominous, pitch emanated from his lips.

"What, what is it, Joey?"

"Today," the voice came from somewhere far away, "he comes for you."

ii

"Yeah, sure I remember the psycho that jumped the band playing here."

"Any idea who he is, or what he was here for?" Jake Hanssen inquired, sliding the picture of Nathan back in his pocket.

"Hell no, probably just some drunk that didn't make the big time and wanted to take it out on someone who was doing all right for himself."

Hanssen nodded to the owner of the nightclub, pretty certain that this was going nowhere.

"He must have been one of those guys that just gets obsessed," the owner continued. "I mean, he was screaming at poor Joey like he knew all about him—gave me the creeps."

Hanssen, who had been about ready to thank the man for his time and leave, looked curiously at Anton Lefebvre, then back to the owner. "You say it almost seemed as if he knew one of the band members?"

The man shrugged, "Yeah, like I said… obsessed."

"What was the band member's name? The one he knew."

"It was Joey Escario. His band plays here every now and then. He—"

Hanssen held up his hand and looked towards Lefebvre. "I know that name."

"Well, sure," the owner proceeded. "He has the potential to be one of the best drummers around... well maybe, *did...*"

Hanssen's eyes lit up as he achieved a mental breakthrough. "He was the damned drummer! The drummer in the Freeman kid's band!"

Hanssen looked back to the owner. "Where can I find Joey Escario?"

A somewhat saddened look came across the owner's face. "Well actually, the whole thing must have shaken him up quite a bit. Joey overdosed that night, and they put him in one of those nut houses. I always thought he had something of a death wish, but still—"

"A psychiatric center?" Hanssen blurted out abruptly.

"Well, yes."

"Which one?" Hanssen was growing extremely anxious.

"He's down at Beth Chaverim Psychiatric Center, but I hear he's—"

But before the man could finish his sentence, Hanssen and Lefebvre had slipped out the door.

iii

Siro Scribner made the last few adjustments to the headline for tomorrow morning's *The Signs of the Times*. It read:

```
JIMI T. EXPO - 4 DOWN, 1 TO GO!
```

Siro had gotten the word from Jimi T. himself that morning, stating that he had selected a guitar player for his band. Joshua Ellwood, perhaps the finest classical guitarist since Segovia, would play for Jimi T.'s yet unnamed band. An interesting pick indeed—not a rock-and-roller at all.

Jimi T. had also told him that his final selection would be made by the end of the week, and then the band would head off, probably to some obscure hideaway, and produce the sound of the Modern Age.

Things were coming together—coming together real good. Siro was at the top of his profession, the world was starting to get a clue as to the meaning of existence, and he even had a new woman in his life—this one with some serious potential.

It doesn't get any better than this.

Siro smiled as he pulled a small vial out of his pocket, twisted the top, inverted it, and snorted himself halfway to Nirvana.

iv

Father Daniel Ananias stood before the icon of Our Lady of Czestochowa. It was by far his favorite image of the Blessed Mother. He gazed upon the scratches—one across the throat and two on the cheek. The first was reportedly the result of a Tartar arrow in the fifteenth century, the other two from a robber's sword. Despite many attempts to repair the image, the "injuries" would remain. The icon itself was of unknown origin, though tradition had attributed it to the evangelist known as Luke.

He had wept deeply at the death of Vanya Ciotola. Serving her funeral, as well as that of the wife and two daughters of his friend, Hugh Jennings Lang, had taken a toll on him these past months.

Father Daniel had recalled that there had been seven names on the chalice from his vision years ago. Now one, Vanya, was gone. Had he failed in the mission he had been given?

Of the other names, he was confident that "Annie" referred to Annie D. Nesterov, and he continued to meet with and console her, and of course, intercede for her in prayer. He found it curious that the senior editor-in-chief of the often-blasphemous publication *The Signs of the Times* held the name Siro, another name on the chalice. Being that it was such an uncommon name, and it was clear that either way, this man was clearly in need, could it be that he was to pray for him?

Father Daniel had no knowledge of the other four: Paula, Nathaniel, Phineas, and Felipe, though he prayed for them each *in absentia* anyway. He had awoken this morning with a sense that one of these people was to face a great peril this very day.

He again turned his gaze to the Black Madonna.

"Can it not be prevented, Good Mother? Can it not be restrained?"

21

"I know what I am fleeing from,
but not what I am in search of."

– Michel de Montaigne

i

"They have laid a trap for him, and I fear that he will not be able to escape from it," Hanoch stated as he walked with Brother Eli along the city streets, apparently unseen by all others around them.

"Then so it must be," Eli responded.

"We were told to protect him."

"And protect him we shall, but only if the boy asks for it."

"That is not what was spoken," Hanoch asserted.

"Explicitly, no. But he is free to choose, and the choice *must* be his. We must have faith that *Elohim* has chosen wisely."

"You know he is defenseless without us," Hanoch petitioned. "And that he will be too confused to beseech our assistance."

"Then there is nothing we can do, and he risks being lost for all eternity."

"So much rests on this boy."

Brother Eli nodded solemnly. "Yes, but lest we forget, this is not our primary calling—our primary purpose. Regardless of the boy's decision, we must progress along this path that has been laid for us."

The two continued to walk, and the scene changed to one of barren desert—the outskirts of the Holy Land. Brother Eli looked to Hanoch as the scene changed one last time to high above Mount Moriah. Both allowed their previous worries to slip from their thoughts for the moment.

"They are coming, my old friend," Eli stated as he looked out across the Holy Land.

Hanoch nodded as his eyes filled up. "It will be good to see the tribes uniting again. I have so missed our people…"

ii

"What the hell happened to you back there, Simon?" Nathan asked angrily as they walked out of the secured part of the facility.

Simon did not look up as the two stepped into the elevator. For a moment it appeared as if he would speak, but then said nothing. Simon began absentmindedly rubbing his artificial hand as if it… *ached.*

Nathan shook his head as the two exited the elevator and headed towards the front doors when…

With a clear sense of urgency, Jake Hanssen and several other men stepped through the automatic doors.

Nathan froze for a just an instant, but it was long enough for he and Hanssen to lock eyes. Hanssen was the first to react.

"GET THEM!" he commanded, pointing directly at the pair.

"Shit!" Nathan shrieked, as he and Simon bolted for the back door.

Hanssen brought his two-way radio to his mouth while running after his prey. "They're trying to slip through the back alley! Bring the car around and have the men cordon off the area!"

Nathan and Simon busted through the emergency exit, setting off the hospital's fire alarm. They sprinted down the alleyway, jumping over cartons and trashcans littered along their escape route. All thoughts of Joey had ceased. Now all Nathan could think of was survival.

Amidst the clanging of the alarm, they could hear a multitude of shuffling feet, accompanied by various shouts. It seemed as if an entire battalion was converging upon them. Nathan and Simon reached the back street just as a car came screeching around the corner.

"We've got to split up!" Simon yelled.

Nathan jerked his head towards Simon, stunned by the suggestion, which seemed so uncharacteristic. "What?"

"We've got to split up, or they'll get us both!"

Nathan did not have a moment to think. Simon bolted into another alleyway straight ahead, while Nathan had only an instant to assess his situation. The car accelerated toward him. Simon was trying to save his own hide, and Nathan could hardly blame him.

With no time to spare, Nathan turned and sprinted to his right. He was sure he could reach the next alleyway before the vehicle reached him. He heard the grinding of the engine as he dove into the side alleyway. The car scraped the walls as it missed its human target by no more than a meter.

He got up and resumed his flight. The sound of multiple footfalls on the pavement penetrated his auditory senses as he scaled a three-meter wall and...

"Come to me, Nathaniel."

The voice slipped into his mind ever so slightly. Still, Nathan was somehow certain its origin was not from within his own thoughts. He fell to the ground, slightly disoriented by the voice, and as he got up he saw someone slip out of his vision just around the corner up ahead.

It was a young boy.

Somehow—he wasn't sure exactly how—but somehow Nathan knew that his only chance of survival rested on his ability to follow this boy, follow him to... to... *safety.*

He stood and stole a brief glance behind him before taking off in the direction of the fleeting vision of the young boy.

iii

Joey smiled, spit, and drooled as he swung his head violently from side to side. The fire alarm was aggravating him greatly. Furthermore, it appeared as if the sprinkler system in the hallway had been triggered. Staff members ran up and down the hallways, most certainly responding to the screams of their terrified patients.

He continued to thrash his head back and forth, but then stopped suddenly. His eyes locked on his doorway, where he saw the droplets of water from the sprinkler seem to slow, taking a more leisurely approach to reaching the floor.

The alarm had lowered in pitch and now maintained a discernibly longer space in between bursts. A staff member galloped slowly past his room, a look of terror in his eyes, momentarily locking his gaze with Joey's.

And then *they* appeared.

As if out of nowhere, two men stood in the doorway. One had a white beard, wore an off-white cassock, and grinned in a manner that sent shivers down Joey's spine. The other wore dark sunglasses and did not smile. Joey knew this person. He had seen him nightly in his dreams.

"Joey, Joey, Joey," the bearded man spoke. "So good to see you!"

Joey bit his lower lip hard out of nervousness. A drop of blood trickled down his chin, where it dangled momentarily before splattering onto his chest. The man with dark shades approached him.

"My dear Joseph, what a predicament they have placed you in here. I speak the truth, do I not?"

Joey nodded slowly, recognizing the subtle yet still unmistakable English accent, but finding himself at a loss for words.

"I never did get the opportunity to thank you for your great work several years back. It was... *most* helpful."

"And most *enlightening!*" the bearded man interrupted, grinning. The man with the shades did not look back at him, but he might as well have. The bearded man cut himself off immediately, and his smile faded.

"My name," the man with the shades continued, "is Jimi T. Expo, and I see I owe you a debt... a debt of gratitude, my good man."

Joey found the words and accent both intriguing, as well as comforting. He hung on every syllable.

"I do have one thing I would like to request of you, however, Joseph, before I offer you whatever you may desire."

"Anything!" Joseph erupted. "Anything for you! Anything!"

A small trace of a smile emerged from the man's face...

22

In a heroic attempt to save those *Čidentūl* led astray by the *Dishalák*, a great life form was brought forth from the *Kóles* into the culture of the *Čidentūl* This life form was called "Abraham", and it was he that established a structure which could evolve, gradually leading many of the *Čidentūl* back to the dominion of the Spiritual Entity. This structure came to be called "Judaism".

Despite the efforts of *Dishalák* to infiltrate and mislead the Followers of Abraham, the structure of Judaism continued to flourish and grow. And the *Kóles* continued to introduce "connected" life forms, or *Tœsii*[1], into the world of the *Čidentūl,* and these life-forms came to be known as "prophets".

Leviat S: 1-5
Book of Given Truths

[1] Translation approximation, "Channeler" or "Teacher"

i

Alexandre Nesterov watched from a distance as Jake Hanssen entered a vehicle and screeched out of its parking space in front of Beth Chaverim Psychiatric Center. His eyes widened, and he was unable to restrain his anxiousness.

"Follow that car!" he commanded, feeling somewhat absurd using such a cliché.

The limo driver did not take time to mull over the nature of the phrase, and pulled the vehicle out into the road, perhaps a bit too quickly. Another car sideswiped them, crashing into the driver's side and turning the vehicle almost completely around.

"*Golubaya bl'yad!*" Nesterov bellowed.

Felix Amosov did not hesitate; he first checked on the safety of his boss, then got out of the car and motioned to the other two vehicles of Nesterov's men to continue in pursuit of Hanssen. They obliged him immediately.

Alexandre Nesterov began to step out of the limousine when the owner of the vehicle that hit them jumped out.

"You rich mother—" the driver began with a tirade of curses. "That will be the last time you mess with someone you think you can step on!"

The man reached inside his jacket, but that was as far as he got. Felix Amosov shot him four times in the chest, and the man fell back against his vehicle then slumped to the ground. Nesterov appeared unfazed.

"Get back in the limo, Felix," he stated coldly.

As Nesterov spoke to Amosov, his own driver stumbled out of the front seat. His head was gashed, and he appeared very disoriented. Nesterov looked back to Amosov, an expression of exasperation and anger lingering on his face.

"I have it, Alex!" Amosov shouted as he knocked the driver to the curb and climbed into the driver's seat. Nesterov got in the passenger side, and the two sped off.

ii

Nathan continued to sprint down and across the Los Angeles streets, chasing the image of the young boy, who constantly seemed to maintain a block's distance between the two.

"*Come to me, Nathaniel, I will protect you.*"

The voice had grown stronger and more frequent. Nathan was thoroughly perplexed, and he could not confirm whose voice it was he was hearing. He could not even discern if it was male or female. The only person in his life who had ever referred to him as Nathaniel was… was his *mother.*

He turned left at the next corner, following where he had seen the boy turn. He had no way of verifying it, but to Nathan it was clear that the boy and the voice were somehow connected. And the truth of the matter was, at this juncture, he really had no other options.

"I am waiting for you, Nathaniel. They cannot harm you once you are with me."

The voice was strong and reassuring, providing Nathan with a surge of energy that kept him going. He was not sure how far behind him his pursuers were, but he had heard a car on the last street make a tire-screeching turn in his direction.

As he ran into a small grocery store, Nathan saw the boy slip out the back, and an eerie sensation came over him. As he ran past the cash register and towards the back, he realized that nobody seemed to be taking notice of him. On several occasions already, he had come within centimeters of people without them so much as flinching or changing their expression.

He emerged from the back door and turned to see the boy running to his right. As he moved to follow, his mind slipped into thoughts of Simon, wondering if he had been able to elude their pursuers.

"Do not worry, Nathaniel. All will be brought into the fold in time."

iii

Joey slowly and methodically twisted and tied his sheet covers. He was happy now. He knew exactly which direction his life was heading.

In the end, he had been faithful to Jesse. He had felt an incredible wave of forgiveness wash over him just minutes before. His two guests were not too happy with his sudden change of heart, however, and explained to him what he must do.

He began humming a tune. He was not sure exactly where he had heard it, but he was sure it had something to do with Jesse. It slowly came back to him, note-by-note, and then…

He was back on stage. He looked to his right, having finished their last number, and watched as Jesse began to play on the old harpsichord. There was not another sound for kilometers.

Joey looked out at the audience and saw thousands of pale-skinned, hairless people staring back at him. Their flesh hung loosely from their bones, and he realized that their mouths were sewn shut. Still, tragically, he could hear their thoughts.

"Murderer!"

He shook his head to indicate his disagreement. He turned to see both Nathan and Simon staring back at him.

"You gave him my hand!" Simon cried.

"No Simon… I'm sorry… they made me do—"

"You gave him three years of my life, and now he wants my soul," Nathan stated gravely.

Jesse continued to play away at the harpsichord as objects thrown from the audience began to fly at him. One from the horde jumped up on stage and struck Jesse on the head. Jesse fell to the ground, and a light stream of blood trickled down the side of his head. He picked himself back up and attempted to resume playing when another fan, and then another, hopped up onto the stage.

Joey tried to rise from his seat to help Jesse, then realized he was chained to his drum set, which in turn had itself become immobile. He looked to Simon and Nathan in a state of panic.

"Help him!" Joey screamed, as he saw Jesse dragged off the stage and into the horde.

Nathan and Simon looked at each other momentarily, then burst into laughter. Joey yanked at the chains but was unable to break free. He looked into the audience and saw the horde ripping away at Jesse, whom he could no longer recognize. Two young men stood just outside of the melee, both bearing an uncanny resemblance to Jesse. They looked from the ravaging horde up to Joey, no sign of emotion within them. A spot of blood emerged from the chest of the boy on the right, slowly expanding, as the boy on the left produced the slightest trace of a smile. Suddenly, a shadowed figure materialized from behind them, encompassing them, and then they were no more.

The music began to play again, and Joey turned to see the back of an unrecognizable man playing the harpsichord. The man turned, and his blazing red eyes nearly blinded Joey. The bizarre apparition resumed his playing, but not before Joey saw, or *sensed*, him wink.

TRYST

Joey looked to his left and saw the preacher, the one called Tæsír Hoc, looking up at him from where the shadowed figure had stood. His expression of approbation could not be missed. Simon approached the Prophet, fell to one knee, and began weeping. The Prophet put his hand upon Simon's shoulder to console him, but upon his touch, Simon vanished, and his clothes fell to the ground.

Joey then looked back to Nathan, who was now with the red-eyed man. Though the music continued to play, the man was no longer at the harpsichord. He and Nathan were... were *waltzing*.

Joey stood atop his bed, one end of his bed sheet knotted snugly around his neck, leaving no more than a half-meter of slack. The other end was firmly wrapped around the light fixture overhead. He was performing a waltz with thin air.

Not my will...

He struggled, then smiled, as tears streamed down his face. The music was deafening, and it was his turn to dance with the Devil.

Not my...

As the musical piece built to its final crescendo, Joey relented and whispered, "Long live rock..." as he leapt from the bed.

23

Allied Press   ~

TEL AVIV, Israel - In what is being described as "The New Exodus", an estimated five million Jews have initiated a journey from Russia to Israel.

In an unprecedented series of events, King Cyrul of the recently recognized nation of Kurdistan has established a half-kilometer-wide corridor for the Jewish travelers to pass through his country.

It is estimated that 90% of all Jews living in the former Soviet states emigrated to Russia after the restoration of the Soviet Union. The fact that Russia itself did not realign with the newly reconstituted Soviet state provided a refuge for those with still vivid memories of life under the communist regime.

In a time when only the member-states of the United League of Democratic Nations retain formal relations with Israel, anxiety is high among surrounding countries concerning the implications of these recent events.

TRYST

i

Nathan sprinted across the street, still pursuing the boy, who stayed beyond his reach, but the gap was clearly starting to narrow. He had run across the busy traffic several times during his pursuit and surprisingly had always found a clear path, not once hearing the sound of a skidding tire. Yet this intersection would be different.

As he stepped out in full throttle onto the street, without notice, a vehicle struck Nathan from the left, knocking him up onto the hood of the car and against the windshield. He felt his head hit the glass, followed by a sensation of warm fluid covering his forehead. The vehicle screeched to a halt, sending Nathan sprawling off the hood and onto the pavement.

He felt a tremendous throb in his left thigh, so strong that he was unable to catch his breath. He looked across the road and saw the boy standing on the sidewalk and looking back at him without the slightest sign of emotion. He just stood there and watched.

Nathan looked up and saw that he had been hit by a limousine. Someone was getting out of the passenger side, cursing loudly.

"What the kind of *sooka ebnataya*—?"

The man stopped ranting as he looked down, and his eyes locked with Nathan's. Nathan looked back in dismay as a menacing smile began to slide across pleasantly surprised Alexandre Nesterov's face.

"Felix, I believe we have caught ourselves a big one."

Felix Amosov stepped from the car, looking down at Nathan, and then at the audience they were beginning to attract. "Let us get him in the car, Alex, and then get out away from this place."

Nesterov nodded and gazed at Nathan as if he was looking at ice cream. He moved towards his prey, who was pretty much immobilized by now, and began to reach down to grab an arm when...

...out of the corner of his eye he caught sight of the little boy. In an instant, Nathan was forgotten.

"Oh my good Lord..."

"Come on, Alex, we gotta get this piece of—"

Nesterov held up a hand to cut Amosov off. He did not break his gaze from the boy, who looked back at him and slowly began to shake his head.

"I-It cannot..."

Both Amosov and Nathan stared at Nesterov curiously, watching tears begin to trickle down the man's cheeks.

"Come to me now, Nathaniel, and they cannot harm you."

Nathan slowly began to move away from the two, putting all his trust in the voice that spoke to him. Nesterov and his sidekick did not seem to notice. As Nathan stood, he felt a new life seep into his leg. He trotted off slowly as he saw Nesterov fall to his knees, his comrade attempting to support him.

"For the love of God, Alex, what is it? What did you see?"

Nesterov looked up to him, at an utter loss to what was happening, and slowly but clearly choked out the words.

"I-I saw my grandson..."

ii

Don Jackson, a federal agent working out of Los Angeles, slipped his *iBerry* back into his suit coat. He turned to Douglas Vorrals, who was seated with him in the back of the limousine and waiting anxiously.

"Looks like your friends caused quite a commotion. Your man Hanssen just chased the Freeman kid out of a psychiatric facility. Both he and the kid are on foot."

"How far away is it?" Vorrals asked.

"Just a few blocks down actually. I've already got men mobilized and in pursuit. But it seems like Hanssen has garnered himself some extra support."

"How do you mean?"

"Well, you told me he only had a handful of men with him."

"That's right."

"Well, our agents seem to think that there are at least a dozen or so vehicles involved in this pursuit, with several men in each vehicle."

Vorrals shook his head. "I have no idea how he could have gotten that much backup." He looked forward as he realized they were not moving. All he could see were multiple vehicles blocking their way.

"What's going on up there? Why aren't we moving?" he asked.

"I'm sorry, sir," the driver responded. "It appears that another limousine is experiencing some difficulties."

Vorrals, frustrated beyond his ability to cope, opened his door and stepped out of the car. He could barely make out, perhaps almost a quarter kilometer up the street, the driver of a somewhat bashed-up limo helping another man into the front seat. There was a crowd around them, and a police car had just pulled up in front of the limousine.

Vorrals watched as the limousine tried to maneuver around the police car but was unable to do so. The officer left his lights flashing and stepped out of his car, obviously not pleased. He approached the driver's side of the limousine and...

Vorrals saw his body jerk a split second before the sound of gunfire reached him. The officer fell to the ground, and the limousine plowed through the police car. Vorrals looked towards Jackson, who was already reaching for his *iBerry*.

Just then, from behind them, Vorrals heard the screeching of tires. He turned to see two cars nearly collide before accelerating down a back alley.

"It's them!" he said assuredly.

"What?" Jackson responded back, holding the phone to his ear.

Vorrals hit the top of the limousine. "Back there, it's them, I'm sure of it! Let's get moving!"

"But, sir, we've got an officer down in—"

"GET IN THE CAR NOW, JACKSON!"

24

i

Siro Scribner barely moved when the phone first rang. Even though it was the middle of the day, he was still attempting to recover from the super-eight-balls which he had done mercilessly the night before.

TRYST

The phone continued to ring relentlessly, and since his answering machine was out of commission from a "Communal Ceremony" the previous week, he had no such luck as to permit it to intercept the call.

He sat up, feeling his head throb like an unregulated nuclear reactor. He reached onto the coffee table, which was littered with beer bottles, bongs, and various other paraphernalia, and picked up a mirror with a few specks of coke left on it.

"Wh-what's going on?" a half-naked woman huddled in the corner moaned.

Siro rubbed his eyes, "Nothing, Sawlus, something's making noise…"

Siro snorted what was left of the coke, then reached over to pick up the phone.

"H-Hello…?"

He paused for a moment, then his eyes opened wide. "Oh yes… ah… yes, Jimi T.! I apologize, we were just doing some mind expansion over here last night—"

Siro paused again, listening intently to what was being said to him.

"You've selected your final band member? Great! Let me guess, Thor from *Future Shock*, right?"

He allowed the excitement to revive him as he looked across the half-dozen or so other bodies sprawled out across the room. "So then, who is it?"

Siro listened for another moment, simultaneous waves of confusion and indiscernible familiarity running through him. His face fell into an expression of utter mystification.

"*Who?*"

ii

Nathan limped along; now thoroughly exhausted and absolutely sure he would collapse within his next three steps. The bleeding had coagulated on his forehead, though his leg once again began to throb relentlessly. This was a complete nightmare (though almost the plot of a thriller novel), having both the FBI and the Russian Mafia on his tail. In different circumstances, it would be near comical. He did not know which would be worse to be captured by, but he had just about reached the point where he would gladly throw in the towel to either.

"Not much farther now, Nathaniel… I am in here."

Nathan looked up from his bent-over position, hands squarely resting on his knees, and saw the boy at the entrance to a large warehouse. The words "Lighthouse Enterprises" were marked clearly across the side of the building. The boy beckoned to him, stood there a moment longer, then disappeared inside.

Nathan staggered forward, listening to the sirens in the background, as well as the unmistakable intermittent sound of skidding tires. They were all after him, he was sure of it. The game was coming to an end.

As he trudged with difficulty toward the warehouse, his mind slipped to thoughts of his mother and father. Far from perfect, they had tried to do their best, and look what it got them.

Nathan felt that they knew that day would come, however. But could they have foreseen his own demise?

"Do not despair, Nathaniel. For I am here with you."

Nathan staggered through the entranceway and found himself standing in a giant, empty warehouse. Empty, save for the boy sitting cross-legged in the center.

Nathan staggered towards him, feeling on the verge of a complete emotional collapse. He just wanted it to end, and the sooner the better.

He stopped in font of the boy, who looked up to him with eyes more like an old man than a six-year-old child.

"Who… who are you?" Nathan asked, his voice audibly quivering.

The boy stood, not releasing his stare from Nathan. "Who *I* am is of little consequence. It is for you that the banquet has been prepared."

Nathan detected just a hint of familiarity in the boy's voice but dismissed it as nothing more than his defeated mind playing tricks on him. As he stood there, he watched the boy's face change, melting into another shape, and then Nathan was looking at an image of himself at a younger age. The boy laughed as he shifted through several more familiar appearances.

"It's easy," the boy said. "Once you connect with the *Kôles*."

Nathan looked amazed, recognizing the source of that word. "Th-Then you're with *The Way?*"

"The one and only."

"And Mystic Realism isn't just a bunch of bull… ahh… crap?"

The boy laughed, and his entire image fluttered and grew. When he came back into focus, Nathan was staring at his mother.

"Now, Nathaniel, you know your mother doesn't like that kind of language."

Nathan's eyes grew wide. "Stop it! Stop screwing with me!"

The boy resumed his previous form, and only then did Nathan notice the crystal that hung from his neck. When the light hit it just right, it produced an image of the Seal, the symbol of Mystic Realism.

At that moment, the sound of multiple cars screeching to a halt broke the conversation. Nathan could hear car doors open and slam, the sound of footfalls, and metal on metal.

Loading weapons, no doubt.

He maintained his gaze on the boy, frightened, but at the same time ready to end this nightmare. The boy showed no indication of fear, and instead smiled at him.

"Well, I gotta go, Nate ol' boy. Got a friend to meet."

"You're not staying to protect me?" Nathan shrieked.

The boy produced a curious look. "Sorry, Nate, this is *your* party. I wasn't invited."

With that, the boy's image blurred, and he transformed into a raven. It cawed, circled once around Nathan's head, and flew off out an opened window on the second level.

"Be not afraid, Nathaniel."

Nathan turned around as a dozen or so men entered the north side of the warehouse. He immediately raised his hands. "I give up… really… I give up…" He began to cry.

The last person through the door was none other than Jake Hanssen. The agents approached Nathan cautiously, obviously not comfortable with the openness of the area. Another few agents entered through the south entrance, and the entire group slowly converged on Nathan.

Within seconds, they were in a circle around him, all pointing weapons directly at him.

"Wait," Hanssen called out. He walked through the circle, slowly, methodically, and stepped to within one meter of Nathan.

"Well, well, Mr. Freeman. You've really been causing me quite a bit of pain."

Nathan kept his hands up. "I-I figured you'd be in jail by this time."

Hanssen smiled, but it was a strained smile. "I'm sure if you had it your way I'd have gotten the chair. But fortunately, I had other plans." Hanssen paused, slipping into a deeper thought. "I am curious though, and I've been wondering this for quite some time. Give me the right answer, and I might let you live. Could you explain to me exactly why you killed your best friend's old lady?"

"What?"

"Yeah, you know, Vanya... or, ahh... Mrs. Storm."

"She's dead?" Nathan asked in astonishment.

Hanssen suddenly found himself trying to prevent the sliver of doubt which had entered his mind from reaching his face. But before he could perform this feat, another voice entered the arena.

"Very convincing, young Nathan. Play the fool and get off scot-free. Seemed to work well for Mr. Hanssen here."

Both Hanssen and Nathan turned to see none other than Alexandre Nesterov walking toward them. At least two-dozen men, these one's with automatic weapons, surrounded the small circle of Hanssen's men with their own, more ominous circle.

"Drop your weapons!" Felix Amosov commanded.

"No!" Hanssen contradicted. He looked at Nesterov dead in the eye. "You don't want to do this, Nesterov. You've got a pending indictment on you, and... and I can help you with that if you just back off."

Nesterov smiled lightly. "Oh, can you, Mr. Hanssen?"

"Sure I can. I'll just make some calls down at the Bureau—"

"Seems to me," Nesterov interrupted, "that you no longer work for the Bureau. I admire you, however, for going to such great lengths to protect young Nathan here. I know he has not been all that cooperative with your Witness

Protection Program."

"Protect him…?"

"FEDERAL AGENTS! EVERYBODY STAND WHERE YOU ARE, DROP YOUR WEAPONS, AND PUT YOUR HANDS UP!"

All eyes looked upward at the sound of the bullhorn. Perhaps fifty agents stood on the upper-deck walkway, surrounding all who were below with rifles aimed and ready. Hanssen and his men were able to recognize Douglas Vorrals and his supposed cavalry.

Weapons from below were now both pointed at each other as well as at select agents up top.

"Well look who has come to the party," Nesterov remarked. "Fancy meeting you here, Douglas."

Hanssen's eyes narrowed as he glanced from Nesterov back to Vorrals. He couldn't miss the momentary expression of discord on the director's face. However, a moment later, it was gone.

"I SAID DROP YOUR WEAPONS!"

Nobody did as they were told. Nesterov turned gently towards Pavel Radchikov. "Pavel, would you do me the kindness of pointing your gun directly at the man with the big mouth up there? I think he is being quite rude, and I may ask you to shut him up, and perhaps have him think twice about asking his men to fire upon us."

Vorrals lowered his bullhorn. "Don't be foolish, Nesterov! We can end this all right now!"

"Such formality, Douglas!" Nesterov called back. "Yet I would tend to agree with you. One way or another, all will end here today."

"Don't even think about it…" It was Hanssen's voice, and Nesterov turned to realize that Hanssen's semiautomatic pistol was now pointing at his head. Instantly, Hanssen became aware of several guns shifting in his direction. He did not have the luxury of seeing the look of curiosity that now rested on Vorrals' face.

Nesterov smiled. "I guess this is what you Americans call a Mexican stand-off. Frankly, it is not all I would have hoped it to be."

Save the cavalier nothing-to-lose attitude of Nesterov, the tension was at a high, and Nathan could see the sweat beginning to trickle down the side of Hanssen's face. Nathan glanced towards Nesterov, then the man with the bullhorn, then suddenly felt dizzy, as one word hit his mind like a bullet.

"NOW!"

Nathan had no idea who shot first, and probably never would. As he dropped to the ground, he saw the man with the bullhorn's body jolt then fall over the second level railing and hit the cement floor. Bullets continued to fire away, ricocheting and echoing throughout the warehouse.

Nathan closed his eyes tightly, instinctively covering his head with his hands. An instant later, amidst the deafening sound, he attempted to open his eyes...

"No, Nathaniel, I am not finished yet."

He then heard another sound enter the melee, one that was more akin to electricity than any firearm he had ever heard.

Nathan gathered himself into the fetal position in the middle of the shooting arena, waiting for his lights to go out permanently...

...but then everything went silent. Nathan assumed that was it, and he had departed from that world of tremendous pain. He had to admit, he wholeheartedly welcomed the end. But then a sound interrupted his thought stream.

"Nathaniel."

Nathan slowly, cautiously looked up. The first thing he noticed was the multiple bodies lying still on the ground surrounding him, trails of blood starting to flow in every direction. Some were clearly riddled with bullets. But others were... *charred.* He saw Hanssen, and Nesterov, and...

A man was standing in the doorway. Nathan could not discern any of his features, as the light shone in brightly from behind him, providing an almost angelic display. Nathan stood, realizing that, save himself and this 'angel', all the others were dead. Not one even did as much as twitch.

The figure approached him, and Nathan was able to begin distinguishing a few features. His hair was jet-black, and he possessed a somewhat muscular build. He wore black denim jeans, a T-shirt, black boots and riding gloves. Most noticeable were his old-style dark sunglasses, which masked any expression that Nathan could even attempt to discern.

The man stepped to within three meters of Nathan, who was now utterly dumbfounded. "Seems like you went through quite a ride to get here, my good friend."

Nathan shook off a brief sense of *déjà vu*, but still felt as if he was on the verge of slipping back into a permanent, and now not altogether unwelcome, unconscious state. The man spoke with a slight English accent, in a voice that was uncannily familiar.

"W-Was it you all along? Were you the one who… who called to me?" Nathan asked.

A gentle smile spread across the man's face. "Yes, Nathaniel. I am."

Nathan noticed the crystal that hung from the man's neck. It was the same as the boy had worn.

He looked about him and then back up at the man. "Th-Then I guess I owe you my life."

The smile widened as the man held his hand out. "Let's hope it doesn't come to that. Let me introduce myself to you. My name is Jimi T. Expo…"

25

And it came to pass that the greatest of all *Tæsir*, the very quintessence of the Spiritual Entity, came into being in the tangible world. This life form was known as "Jesus", and it was for Him to lead the *Čidentîl* into the ways of the Spiritual Entity, and incite their subsequent assimilation into the *Kôles*.

But, alas, this was not to be, as the *Ďishalák* deceived the life form known as Jesus, setting Him at odds with the very Followers of Abraham that He had come to save. In a tragic event spurred by the workings of the *Ďishalák*, the life form known as Jesus was prematurely terminated. It was at this time that the *Ďishalák* instituted the greatest scourge upon the tangible world ever imagined. This affliction came to be known as "Christianity".

Leviat W: 1-6
Book of Given Truths

i

Andrey Gavrilenkov stood just inside the back entrance of Chef Volo's Italian Restaurant in Atlantic City, trying to appear as if he was waiting his turn for the men's room. He had spotted Mikhail Ostankino, smoking away at a table while seemingly having a grand old time with none other than Mikey Logiarato, Nesterov's only competition (though a friendly one) for the position of the most powerful syndicate boss in North America.

TRYST

What a quaint little tryst!

There were few things worse than disloyalty, in Andrey's mind. So being designated the task of "whacking" the traitor called Ostankino would be a true labor of love. He had never understood Nesterov's brief and seemingly unconditional reconciliation with the man. Sure, business was business, but nothing ever trumped family.

Logiarato would no doubt be irritated at having his dinner interrupted by a hit job, but he was still a true wise-guy, and understood the importance of properly settling a score. His forgiveness would be assured.

Andrey reached inside his suit jacket to grab hold of his miniature Magfly 179 (with built in silencer), when his *iBerry* phone vibrated.

He hesitated, then recognized the vibration rhythm of the phone to be that of his daughter.

Not now!

A million thoughts shot through Andrey's head. Sascha had left her fiancé after their last "incident", and had already taken a liking to some new guy—a bit younger than the previous punk, and seemingly a decent man. Andrey did not like the fact that this one was into that new-fangled religious fashion, but he felt comfortable that it would be just a short-lived phase. The odds seemed against this call being an emergency, but he could not let it go. He turned away from the dining area toward the back door and picked up.

"Honey, it is not a good time, is everything—?"

"I am sorry to interrupt you, sir. Is this the father of Sascha Lenuscka Gavrilenkov?"

Andrey's stomach dropped. "It is. What are you—?"

"My name is Ralph Tobit, and I'm a paramedic. I first want to tell you that I believe your daughter will be okay, but she has taken an overdose…"

Mikhail Ostankino felt his heart begin to race as he crushed out his cigarette. He sat across the table from the man whom he would kill within the next sixty seconds, taking the final step in ascending to the title of most powerful organized crime figure in North America. A well-placed explosive device in Alexandre Nesterov's cottage would see to it that good ol' Alex's lights would be put out permanently once he returned from whatever excursion he was currently on. Sure, there would be the little matter of cleaning up a few of Nesterov's loyalists, but that would be mere piece-work for some lower-level men in his syndicate.

The ever-fattening Mikey Logiarato continued to bellow out another poorly told Italian joke, when Mikhail's eye was suddenly caught by movement at the back of the restaurant—right where his planned exit was to be. He attempted to subtly glance over and saw none other than Andrey Gavrilenkov, looking quite agitated as he spoke into his phone.

The gods must be smiling on me! Mikhail mused excitedly. *This could be a two-for-one deal!*

He glanced back to Logiarato. If Mikhail was to have his whole enchilada, now was the time. As Logiarato belly-laughed at his own punch line, Mikhail reached his right hand under the table, touching the pistol that one of his men had attached to the underside when...

Something in his mind switched. Mikhail suddenly felt encompassed by a presence—one he could only describe as *maternal*—which froze him in his seat.

Logiarato, seeing the complete transformation in his guest's face, stopped laughing. "Mikhail? What's wrong? You Ruskies don't like my jokes?"

Mikhail struggled against the presence as he looked over to see Gavrilenkov terminate his call and hasten out the back door.

Not now! Mikhail cried out in his mind. *Get out of my head!*

Then from within the presence, he heard—he sensed—a voice. It was a voice he did not recognize, yet which was clearly familiar nonetheless.

"You must cease this course of action, Mikhail," the motherly voice commanded. *"For it is these very men from whom you will seek aid in the dark time to come."*

Mikhail grabbed his head as he shrieked aloud, "Get out of my head!" Then standing from the table, he bolted out the back door, leaving behind the perplexed Logiarato.

ii

Simon stumbled along the sidewalk, thoroughly exhausted from the chase. It was nightfall now, and he slowly staggered up the steps of the enormous cathedral-like building, the words "MYSTIC REALISM" engraved over the entranceway.

He staggered inside and saw the cleric standing at the altar, his back to Simon.

"Enter, my son," the cleric called out.

Simon limped up the aisle, realizing that the church—was it really a church?—was completely empty, save himself and the cleric. He reached the front pews before the altar, and the teacher turned around, smiling.

"Great Teacher..." Simon whispered.

"Yes, my son," the man called Tæsír Hoc responded.

Simon looked down, as if about to cry, but then turned his stare back to the Prophet.

"I-I did as you asked. I brought him to you."

"Yes," the Prophet responded. "Yes, my son. That you did. And I can assure you, your rewards for such a deed will be both immense and eternal."

Simon nodded quietly, his lower lip quivering slightly. "Y-You promised me..."

The Prophet looked at him inquisitively, feigning ignorance. "I promised you...?"

Simon sniffled and wiped his eyes with his left hand, nodding. He was struggling not to cry, and slowly held up his artificial hand.

"Oh! Oh yes, my son. How could I be so foolish? Why of course! You would like to have your hand back in exchange for your undying servitude to the *Kôles*. Is that correct?"

Simon clenched his eyes shut, allowing a few tears to spill, and nodded.

"Well, very well then. I don't think *that* should be a problem at all. You know, my son, I've really got to hand it to you... oops! I said 'hand' in a most inappropriate fashion, did I not? I am so sorry. Could you ever find it in your heart to forgive me?"

Simon looked to the Tæsír with eyes now full of tears. "Teacher, I..."

The Prophet held a single finger up to his lips. "Shhhhh, be still, my pupil. You have been a good servant, and I shall give you your reward. Now..."

He reached out; placing both hands around Simon's artificial limb, he bowed his head. Simon stared longingly at the Prophet, whose lips moved silently.

At that moment, he suddenly felt a surge of energy sweep through him, though it was not devoid of pain. He cried out.

"AAAAAAAAAAAAAHHHHHHHH!"

"Be still, my son! For it is the Life-Force that flows through you!"

Simon fell to his knees, asking, *begging,* for the pain to subside, and finally it obliged. The Prophet released his grip, and Simon collapsed to the floor.

A moment later, Simon stirred, gently pulling himself up to stand.

"The *Kôles* has granted you a tremendous gift, my brother."

Simon stared at the Prophet curiously and then jerked his palm up to his face.

It's real!

He manipulated his fingers, made a fist, and began to giggle. The Prophet smiled back at him.

Simon continued to laugh as he began to turn his hand, then stopped abruptly. There, on the back of his hand, was the Seal.

"Consider that, my brother, a bonus for your services."

Simon looked up at the Prophet, troubled, and at a loss as to what to say. Yet his concern quickly faded as thoughts of new possibilities danced in his head. He could make *music* again. He could...

"Well, young Simon, I do believe that this calls for a celebration, would you agree?"

Simon looked up to the Prophet, slowly feeling his energy creep back. "Y-Yes, Great Teacher."

Tæsír Hoc nodded as he reached out, firmly grasped Simon's new hand, and led him up to the altar. He opened a cabinet behind the altar, pulled out a large bottle of tequila and two double-shot glasses, and placed them on the altar.

Simon eyes widened. "Oh no, Great Teacher... I can't... I haven't had a drink in five—"

"Are you not grateful for the gift that the *Kôles* has bestowed upon you, my brother?"

TRYST

Simon shook his head quickly, apologetically. "No... No, Great Teacher, it's just that—"

"Do you feel it is proper to accept a gift, and not provide a simple gratuity in return?"

"Great Teacher, I—"

"We serve the *Kôles*! She is within us, and we within Her! The *Kôles* provides us with so much, yet asks us so little in return. Do not fear, Simon! I am sure that one drink will not spoil your precious sobriety binge!"

Simon looked down, shaking his head apologetically. "No, Great Teacher, I guess it would not."

Tæsír Hoc smiled. "Very well then!" he exclaimed with delight, and poured them both a drink. They toasted each other, and while the Prophet consumed his drink in one swipe, it took Simon slightly longer.

Simon put the glass down and coughed. The Tæsír laughed, patting him on the back. "Old habits die hard, do they not, my brother?"

Simon nodded, taking in a full breath of air, and smiled weakly. It was not as bad as he thought. In fact, he was feeling somewhat... somewhat invigorated at the moment. Like he could conquer any battle, any nation, any...

"Another, my brother?" the Prophet asked, already pouring the tequila into the second shot glass.

Simon was about to once again provide his standard, learned response to the offer, but hesitated. This really *was* a once in a lifetime occasion. He had gotten his hand back... everything was looking up, and that last drink was so... so *refreshing*. Surely one more wouldn't...

"Simon?"

He looked up to see the Prophet holding his glass out to him. After another brief pause, he reached for the glass, feeling a tad bit guilty, but knowing he would get over it.

"Bottoms up?"

Citations

Chap	Reference
	Unknown (Uncredited Folktale) *Appointment in Samarra*. Oldest version is recorded in the Babylonian Talmud, Sukkah 53a.
1	Eliot, Thomas Stearns. *The Hollow Men, Poems: 1909-1925*, T.S. Eliot, 1925.
5	Unknown. Credited as both an Egyptian Proverb and a Jewish saying.
14	The Duke of Brunswick. Letter from the Grandmaster of German Freemasonry recommending the dissolution of the entire organization, due to the fact that he felt is had been infiltrated and was being manipulated by "unseen hands", 1794.
17	Freud, Sigmund. "Hero-Worship", *Mourning and Melancholia*. Hogarth Press, 1955.
18	Smedes, Lewis B. (1921-2002). *The Art of Forgiveness*, Lewis B. Smedes, Ballantine books/Random House, 1996.
21	de Montaigne, Michel Eyquem (1533-1592).

For additional information on authors, artists, works, and quotes cited in *Dominion* (including the ability to purchase) please visit www.thedominionproject.com/citations.html .

The Dominion Project continues with Book IV

REQUIEM

Compassing Song

A year of unmitigated seclusion for the members of the Mystic King's band has come to an end, as *Çön Razón*, the musical coterie for the emerging age, steps back onto center stage. Nathaniel Freeman-Page, the band's composing aficionado, has discovered everything he ever dreamed of, though in the rare opportune moments of quiet and solitude, tormenting visions of Jesse cause him to question the cost of his newfound life of indulgence. With Siro Scribner and his associate and lover Sister Sawlus leading the informational charge, the progressively conflict-free world ponders the question: Has the belief in a personal deity been the cause of all of mankind's struggles? Could *The Way of Mystic Realism* indeed be the final requiem of religion and its god as we know it?

Order your copy at
www.thedominionproject.com

Also available: ***Dominion Interlude: Reader's Companions***
with character sketches, book summaries, references and more!

Direct Ordering of the Dominion Series

Especially for those who do not have online access, all books can be purchased direct from T.C.C./Sacrata Dei Press by mail.

Dominion – The Series

Dominion – Reference

For the Dominion reading enthusiast who wishes to delve deeper into the series, these brief reader's companions/reference are a helpful tool providing character profiles, time and location references, summaries, background, and descriptions. Each Interlude is meant to follow its corresponding book from the series, offering a more in-depth understanding of the "Dominion world" while further preparing the reader for the next book.

Please call (574) 307-0413 for current mailing address, shipping rates, and tax rates (where applicable). Once obtained, please identify in your mailing your name and address, which book(s) you are ordering and the quantity, and provide a check or money order in U.S. dollars made payable to T.C.C./Sacrata Dei Press.